The Best Adirondack Stories of Philander Deming

New York Classics
Frank Bergmann, Series Editor

Philander Deming.
Courtesy of The Adirondack Museum.

The Best Adirondack Stories of Philander Deming

Philander Deming

With a Foreword by Frank Bergmann

Syracuse University Press

Copyright © 1997 by Syracuse University Press
Syracuse, New York 13244-5160

All Rights Reserved

First Edition 1997
97 98 99 00 01 02   6 5 4 3 2 1

This book is published with the assistance of a grant from the John Ben Snow Foundation.

The paper used in this publication meets the minimum requirements of American National Standard for Information Sciences—Permanence of Paper for Printed Library Materials, ANSI Z39.48-1984. ♾

Library of Congress Cataloging-in-Publication Data
Deming, P. (Philander), 1829–1915.
  The best Adirondack stories of Philander Deming / Philander Deming ; with a foreword by Frank Bergmann.
      p. cm. — (New York classics)
  Contents: Lost — Willie — Ike's wife — John's trial — An Adirondack neighborhood — An Adirondack home — The court in Schoharie — Tompkins — Mr Toby's wedding journey — In slavery days.
  ISBN 0-8156-0442-4 (cloth : alk. paper)
  1. Adirondack Mountains Region (N.Y.)—Social life and customs—Fiction.   2. Mountain life—New York (State)—Adirondack Mountains   Region—Fiction.   I. Title.
II. Series.
PS1534.D4A6   1997
813'.4—dc20   96-43635

Manufactured in the United States of America

Contents

Foreword by Frank Bergmann vii

Lost 1

Willie 15

Ike's Wife 26

John's Trial 40

An Adirondack Neighborhood 57

An Adirondack Home 79

The Court in Schoharie 105

Tompkins 128

Mr. Toby's Wedding Journey 150

In Slavery Days 174

Foreword

Long before I became seriously interested in the literature of upstate New York, I came across one of Philander Deming's Adirondack stories. It was "Lost," judged good enough by Harry R. Warfel and G. Harrison Orians to have made their outstanding anthology *American Local-Color Stories* (1941), and included there as the only selection from New York State. Later on, I was reacquainted with—in fact, more widely and thoroughly introduced to—Deming's work by Thomas F. O'Donnell's writings on upstate literature (some of which are now conveniently available in *Upstate Literature,* see below). In addition to *Adirondack Stories* (1880), I now read *Tompkins and Other Folks* (1885) and *The Story of a Pathfinder* (1907). I found in most of these stories an astutely observant eye, a sparse but finely honed style, and a reluctance to prettify or editorialize—in sum, qualities I had come to prize in the works of the great American realist writers from the Civil War onward. I was tempted to assign some of Deming's sketches in my American literature classes, but the price of the reprints was too steep: even now, the three books will set you back a combined $82.50, before taxes.

It was, then, with great pleasure that I saw Ted Comstock list *Adirondack Stories* as number ten in his "guide to 25 of the most collectible Adirondack titles" ("Special Editions," in *Adirondack Life* [Nov./Dec. 1988, 54–57]; Comstock's number nine is Charles Dudley Warner's *In the Wilderness,* reprinted in the present series in 1990). His endorsement of "the grittiest stories ever written about the Adirondacks" pointed to a readership beyond the college classroom and was certainly instrumental in the decision by Syracuse University Press to publish Deming's best work in one affordable volume.

As the title of the present selection indicates, the Adirondacks are Deming's focus. The first five stories are from *Adirondack Stories* directly, but "Tompkins" and "An Adirondack Home" (from *Tompkins*) and even "In Slavery Days" (from *Pathfinder*) also relate to that majestic wilderness. They are complemented by two stories from *Tompkins* that go farther south, "Mr. Toby's Wedding Journey," with its Irvingesque glimpse of the Catskills, and "The Court in Schoharie," a lovely vignette of bucolic life in the valley of that tributary of the Mohawk. In arranging the entries, I have put four often sad but never maudlin pieces first, followed by three much sunnier autobiographical ones. Three finely balanced human interest stories conclude the volume; the last of these, "In Slavery Days," is an extended comment on racial prejudice, quite as moving and courageous as Kate Chopin's terse and much better known "Désirée's Baby."

Deming was born on February 6, 1829, in Carlisle, not far from the Schoharie river, but his father's assignments as a minister soon took the family up into Franklin County. After preparing for college at the Whitestown Seminary, Deming distinguished himself at the University of Vermont (1861). In 1872, he graduated from Albany Law School but continued his career as a court reporter, a profession he significantly improved by introducing verbatim reporting through stenography (his handbook *The Court Stenographer* appeared in 1879). His formative years and his experiences in court furnished the subject matter for his sketches, in many of which Adirondack residents are shown as leading exacting lives amid the demanding mountains "Adirondack" Murray had glorified in 1869 for the benefit of tourists. Deming's serious, realistic vein was quickly tapped by William Dean Howells for *The Atlantic Monthly* for several years from 1873 on. Deming retired in 1882, and his biographer found telling words for those final years: "In later life he was a striking figure on the streets of Albany, because of his abundant white hair and his deeply lined face. He resembled portraits of Franz Liszt. He was highly esteemed, yet few knew him intimately. He never married." Deming died in Albany on February 9, 1915.

In addition to the biographical sketch by Louie M. Miner in *Dictionary of American Biography* (1946, 5:231–32), the following discussions of Deming and his work make good reading: F. L. Pattee, *The Development of the American Short Story* (1923), 269–71; Abe C. Ravitz, "Philander Deming: Howells' Adirondack Prodigy," *New York History* 36 (Oct. 1955): 404–12; Thomas F. O'Donnell, "The Secret Passion of Philander Deming," NAHO 12 (Winter 1979–80): 13–15; and Kate H. Winter, "North Country Voices," in *Upstate Literature: Essays in Memory of Thomas F. O'Donnell,* ed. Frank Bergmann (Syracuse: Syracuse Univ. Press, 1985), 143–64.

Frank Bergmann

Utica College of Syracuse University
Utica, New York
March 1996

The Best Adirondack Stories of Philander Deming

Lost

He was lost in the edge of the Adirondack Wilderness. It must have been the sound of the flail. "Thud, thud, thud," came the beat of the dull, thumping strokes through the thick, opaque, gray fog. Willie was hardly four years old; and when once he was a few rods away from the barn, off on the plain of monotonous yellow stubble, he could not tell where he was, and could not detect the deceptive nature of the sound and its echo. He could see nothing: whichever way he looked, wherever he walked, there were the same reverberations; and the same narrow dome of watery gray was everywhere shutting close down around him. As he followed the muffled sound, in his efforts to get back to the barn, it seemed to retreat from him, and he ran faster to overtake it. He ran on and on, and so was lost.

That night and the next day a few neighbors, gathered from the adjoining farms, searched for Willie. They wandered about the fields and the margin of the woods, but found no trace of the lost child. It became apparent that a general search must be made.

The fog had cleared away on the second morning

after Willie was lost, as about a hundred woodmen and farmers and hunters, gathered from the farms and forest and settlement near by, called Whiskey Hollow, stood and sat in grotesque groups around the little farmhouse and barn, waiting the grand organization into line, preparatory to sweeping the woods, and finding Willie.

During all the hours of the two previous nights the lanterns and torches had been flashing in and out behind the logs and brush of the fallows; and the patches of snow that lingered in spite of the April rains gave evidence that every foot of the adjacent clearing had been trampled over in the search. But the men were not yet satisfied that the search about the farm had been thorough. Standing by the house, they could see the field of the night's work,—the level stubble of the grain-lot, and the broad, irregular hollow used as pasture, and filled with stumps and logs and brush. Here and there could be seen men still busy poking sticks under the logs, and working around bog-holes in the low ground. "You see it stands to reason," said Jim, addressing a group by the house, "that a little chap less than four years old could not get out of this clearing into the woods."

A white-haired patriarch remarked, with great confidence and solemnity, "The boy is within half a mile of the house; and, if I can have command of six men, I will find him." The patriarch continued to press his suggestion until he secured his company and started off, feeling that he carried a great weight of responsibility. He joined the log-pokers and bog-explorers; but nothing came of his search.

The morning was wearing away: the men, gathered from a great distance, were impatient of the delay to organize the line.

Willie had been out nearly forty-eight hours. Could it be that he had passed beyond the stubble-field into the forest, nearly half a mile from the house? If he had managed to cross the brook at the edge of the woods, he had the vast Adirondack Wilderness before him. It was time to search thoroughly and upon a large scale, if the boy was to be found alive.

But a reason for delay was whispered around,—the fortune-woman was coming. Soon a rough farm-wagon came up the road and through the yard-gate, and stopped in front of the door of the farmhouse. There was a hush of voices, and a reverent look upon the part of some of the men, and a snicker and digging of their neighbors' ribs upon the part of others, as a large, coarse-featured woman was helped out of the wagon by the driver of the team.

This female was the famous fortune-woman. Some of these dwellers on the edge of the wilderness were no better than the classic Greek and noble Roman of ancient times; for they believed in divination.

The fortune-woman went into the house where the mother of Willie sat, crying. The men crowded the room and windows and door. Some of the men looked solemn; some jeered. Out at the door Josh explained apologetically to the unbelievers, that, "inasmuch as some thinks as how she can tell, and some thinks as how she can't, so it were thought better for to go and fetch her, so as that all might satisfactory themselves, and no fault found, and every thing done for the little boy."

After a brief *séance* with the teacup in the house, the fortune-woman, urged by the men, went "out of doors" and walked up along the hollow with her teacup, experimenting to find the child. About half of the men straggled after her. Jim declared to the group who lingered at the house that he would sell out and leave, if the entire crowd disgraced the town by following after that "old she-devil."

To a stranger coming upon the field at this time, the scene was curious and picturesque, and some of it unaccountable. In the background was a vast descending plain of evergreen forest, sloping away from the Adirondack highlands to the dim distance of the St. Lawrence Valley, where could be seen the white, thread-like line of the great river; and still beyond the Canada woods, melting away to a measureless distance of airy blue. In the foreground was a vulgar old woman waddling along, and snatching here and there a teacupful of water from the puddles formed by the melting snow; and fifty vigorous men in awe-struck attitudes were gazing at her, and, when she moved, they followed after.

Odd as this grotesque performance seemed, it had in it a touch of the old heathenish grandeur belonging to the ancient superstitions. The same strange light that through all time has shone from human faces as souls reach after the great infinite unknown shone from the faces of some of these men. There were fine visages among them. Burly Josh and a hunter with dark poetic eyes would have been a match for handsome, pious Æneas or the heroes of Hellas, who watched the flight of birds, and believed in a fortune-woman at Delphos.

But the simple faith of these modern worshippers was not rewarded: after the Greek pattern, the oracle gave ambiguous responses. The old woman proclaimed, with her eyes snapping venomously, that there was "a big black baste astandin' over the swate child." She announced, with a swing of her right arm extending around half a circle, that "the dear, innocent darlin' was somewhere about off that way from the house." She scolded the men sharply for their laziness, telling them they had not looked for the lost child, but were waiting around the house, "while the blessed baby starved, and the black baste stood over him."

Dan caught at this, and declared that the "old hypocrite" was no fool. She knew enough to understand that "it was no way to find a lost boy to shell out a whole township of able-bodied men, and set them to chase an old woman around a lot."

The fortune-woman came back to the house, held a final grand *séance* with the teacup divinity, and declared that the "swate child" was within half a mile of the place, and if they would only look they would find him, and that, if they did not look, within two days "the big black baste would devour the poor, neglected darlin'." After this the fortune-woman was put into the wagon again, and Josh drove her home. It was fully in accordance with the known perversity of human nature, that the faith of the believers in her infallibility was not in the slightest degree shaken.

The company, having been increased by fresh arrivals to more than one hundred men, organized for the search. The colonel ranged the men in line about twenty feet apart, extending across the wide stubble-field and the pasture. The men were directed by the colonel to "dress to the left;" that is, as he explained it, for each to watch the man at the left, and keep twenty feet from him, and observe all the ground in marching.

The word was given, and the line, more than half a mile long, began to move sidewise or platoon fashion, sweeping from the road by the house across the clearing to the woods. It was a grand charge upon the great wilderness. The long platoon, under the instruction of their commander, swept the woods bordering the clearing, and then, doubling back, made semicircular curves, going deeper and deeper at each return into the primeval forest. The limit of their marching and countermarching in one direction was a river too broad to be crossed by fallen trees: it was sure that Willie could not have crossed the river. The termination of the marches in the other direction was controlled by the judgment of the colonel. It was a magnificent tramp through the wild, wet woods, under the giant trees, each eye strained, and expectant of the lost boy. Here and there, in advance of the line as it progressed, a partridge, aroused by the voices of the men, would start from the undergrowth, and trip along for a few steps with her sharp, coquettish *"quit, quit, quit,"* and then whir away to some adjacent hollow, to be soon again aroused by the advancing line.

The afternoon was wearing away. The woods had been thoroughly explored for about two miles from the clearing,—far beyond what it seemed possible for an infant less than four years old to penetrate.

The colonel said he could think of nothing more to be done. The men returned in straggling groups to the farmhouse, tired, sad, hungry, and dispirited. There were many speculations whether Willie could be still alive, and, if alive, whether he could get through another night. "You see," said Josh, "such a *little* feller, and three days and two nights a wettin' and a-freezin' and a-thawin', and no grub: why, he couldn't, don't you see?"

It was never found out, not even at Whiskey Hollow, where the men unveiled all their iniquities, who the wretch was that first started the dark suggestion about the *murder* of little Willie. Dan became very angry when the men, fatigued and famished, straggling back to the farmhouse from the disorganized line, as above narrated, began to hint that "things was tremendous queer," and that "them as lost could find," and that John, Willie's father, was a perfect hyena when he was "mad."

Dan, for the only time that day, became profane as he denounced the sneak, whoever it might be, who had started such a suggestion. He expressed the conviction that the fortune-woman had her foot in it some way. Superstitious fools, he said, were likely to be suspicious.

But Dan's anathemas did not stay the rising tide. As the searchers came back, suspicious glances were turned upon the father, who sat with his afflicted family at the house. Some of the searchers stealthily examined under the barn, believing that Willie had been "knocked on the head" with a flail, and concealed under the floor.

But John the father was no coward, and he had neighbors and friends who believed in him. They told him of the suspicions arising against him. On the instant he called a meeting at the little hovel of a schoolhouse, a few rods down the road. The hundred searchers gathered there, and filled the room, sitting, lolling, and lying upon the benches. The father of the lost child, almost a stranger to most of the searchers, took his place at the teacher's desk, and confronted his accusers.

It was plain, direct work. Here were a hundred men who had exhausted all known means of finding the lost boy; and more than fifty of them had said in effect to the man before them, "We think you killed him." All were looking at John: he rose up, and facing the crowd with a dauntless eye, he made a speech.

If this were a story told by Homer or Herodotus, I suppose John's speech would figure as a wonderful piece of eloquence; for a man never had a grander opportunity to try his strength in persuading others than John had. But in fact there was nothing grand about the matter, except that here was a straightforward man with nerves of steel, who had been "hard hit," as Dan said, by the loss of his boy, and was now repelling with courage, and almost scorn, a thrust that might have killed a weaker man.

His speech was grammatically correct, cool, deliberate, and dignified. He said he had no knowledge of the black-hearted man who had originated so cruel a suspicion at such a time, and he did not wish to know who he was. He asked his hearers to consider how entirely without support in the known facts of the case the accusations were that had been suggested against him. It was a purely gratuitous assumption, with not a particle of evidence of any kind to establish it. He had understood that he was supposed to have killed his child in anger, and then concealed the body. Such a thing could not have happened with him as killing his own child or any other child in that way; and, if it had so happened, he would not have concealed it. He only wished to brand this creation of some vile man, there present probably, as a lie. That was all he had to say upon that point.

In continuing his speech, when he alluded to what he had suffered in losing the boy he loved the best of any thing on earth, there was a twitching of the muscles of his face, which, however, he instantly controlled as unworthy of him. He closed his speech by appealing to his friends who had known him long and well, to come forward at this time, and testify to his integrity.

As he ceased, the men rose up from the benches, and conversed together freely of the probabilities about John. A group of three or four gathered around him, and, placing their hands upon his shoulders, told the crowd that they had known John for twenty years, and that he was incapable of murder, or perfidy, or deceit, and as honest a man as could be found in the county.

It was decided not to search any farther that day, as there was no prospect now that Willie would be found alive. The men went home, agreeing to come again after three days, by which time the sleet and light snow that had fallen would have all melted, and search for the body might be successfully made.

John went to his house. As he met his afflicted family, and realized that little Willie was now gone, that the search was given up, and his child was dead, his Spartan firmness yielded, and he wept such tears as strong, proud men weep when broken on the wheel of life. The last cruel stab at his moral nature and integrity hurt hard. He was a pure, upright man, a church-member, and without reproach.

As the three days were passing away that were to elapse before the search for the body should begin, it became apparent in the community that John's Homeric speech had done no good. The wise heads of Whiskey

Hollow declared, that at the next search there would be, first of all, a thorough overhauling about the immediate premises. Their suspicions found some favor in the community. Some were discussing indignantly, and some with tolerance, the probability of John's guilt. Even good Deacon Beezman, a magistrate who "lived out on the main road," and who was supposed to carry in his own person at least half of the integrity and intelligence of his neighborhood, declared that he would not spend more of his precious time in searching for the boy. He made it the chief point in the case that John "acted guilty." He had noticed that this rustic Spartan sat in his house, and read his newspaper with apparent interest, as in ordinary times, on the day of the last search; and this indifference was evidence of his guilt. It was apparent that any color of proof, if there had been any such thing, might have served as a pretence for an arrest of the afflicted father.

The morning appointed as the time to seek for the body came. The excitement was high; and men came from great distances to join in the exploration.

Eight miles away, up across the river that flowed through the forest, dwelt Logan Bill, a hunter. At an early hour he left his cabin, and took his course down the stream toward the gathering-point. There was an April sun shining; but in the wilderness solitudes it was cold and dreary. He kept along the margin of the stream to avoid the tangle of brush and fallen trees.

At nine o'clock, Logan was still three miles from

John's clearing. He was passing through a hollow where the black spruce and pine made the forest gloomy. He came upon a bundle of clothing; he turned it over: it was Willie!

And thus alone in the wilderness Logan solved the mystery. Through three miles of trackless forest, under the somber, sighing trees of the great woods, through the fog and falling rain and snow, the child had struggled on, feeling its way in the night along the margin of the river, until it grew weak and sick, and fell and died.

There was a choking in Logan's throat as he lifted the cold little body, and carried it onward down the stream, and noted the places where the infant must have climbed and scrambled in its little battle for life. It was a strange two hours to him as he bore the pure, beautiful, frozen corpse toward the settlement.

At eleven o'clock he reached the clearing. He saw the scattered groups of men gathered about John's house and barn. Some of the men seemed to be searching about the barn to find the body of the boy they believed to be murdered. Logan felt his frame tremble, and his temples throb, realizing as he did the weight of life and death wrapped in the burden that he bore. He spoke no word, and made no gesture, but, holding the dead child in his arms, marched directly past the barn to the dooryard, and up in front of the house. There he stopped, and stood and looked with agitated face at the farmhouse door.

The shock of Logan's sudden coming was so great that no one said, "The body is found;" but all the men stopped talking, and some, pale and agitated, gathered in a close huddle around Logan, and looked at the little, white, frosted face, and in hushed tones asked where Logan had found the body.

A blanket was brought, and spread upon a dry place in the yard, and Logan laid his little burden upon it.

John came out, and approached the spot where his little Willie was lying. There was a deeper hush as the crowd made way for the father; and the rough men, some of whom were now crying, looked hard at John "to see how he would take it." John stood and gazed, unmoved and lionlike: not a muscle of his strong face quivered as he saw his boy. He called in a tone of authority for his family to come, and said to his wife in a clear, calm voice, as she came trembling, weeping, fainting, "Mother, look upon your son."

He turned, and surveyed the crowd with the same dauntless eye he had shown in making his Homeric speech at the schoolhouse. To some of the company that eye was now a dagger.

John was cool, calm, and polite. He uttered no reproach, and was kind in his words to all. A half-hour passed. The crowd went away in groups, discussing the amazing wonder, "how ever it could be that such a little feller as Willie could have got so far away from the house."

The next day religious services were held, and in the afternoon little Willie was laid to rest upon a sunny knoll. John wept at the grave. A poisoned arrow was drawn from the strong man's heart, and a great grief was there in its stead.

Willie

It frightened us a good deal when we found the little dead boy. This is the way it was. We were three country lads going home across the lots at noon for our dinner. In passing a lonely pasture-ground we saw a little basket lying ahead of us upon the grass. We made a race for it, and Ed captured the prize; a little farther on, we picked up a small hat, which we at once recognized as Willie Dedrick's. Then we turned the angle of the zigzag rail-fence; and there in the corner, jammed close under the bottom rail, was beautiful little Willie, only five years old.

His clothing was torn and bloody, and he did not move: we felt a little afraid, because he was so still; but we went up to him. He was dead; and his plump little features were all blackened with great bruises.

It shocked us very much. Only three hours before, we had been playing with Willie at the pond. We felt that it was a terrible thing to find him dead in this unlooked-for manner. We asked each other what Walter and Mary would do when they should hear of this: Willie was the only boy they had. And then the question came up what *we* ought to do under such circumstances. There was no one in sight to tell us. It was suggested that we might take up the body, and carry it home to Walter and Mary. It was not far through the lot, and down the bank, to the pond where their home was. It seemed natural and right at first that we should take the chubby little boy, and carry him home. But we shrank from the presence of death, even in the form of little Willie; and, besides that, we had certain dim and confused ideas, as country lads do who read the city newspapers, that somehow a coroner was necessary, and that it would not be lawful or safe for us to meddle with Willie thus strangely found dead from an unknown cause.

So we sat down upon the large stones near by Willie, and held a council. There was no chairman appointed, and no secretary, and none of the surroundings that ordinarily belong to deliberative bodies: nevertheless, in all the essentials of a great council, this occasion was very eminent. Here were three lads seated upon three fragments of the ancient granite which strews the northern slope of the Adirondack Mountains; and below them stretched the wild woods away to the valley of the mighty St. Lawrence; and in their midst, upon that bright summer day, sat the skeleton king, with his awful sceptre and his iron crown, pressing upon their young hearts those matchless terrors which have ruled the world since time began.

It was an august presence; and the boys felt their

responsibility more than members of councils ordinarily do. Their final conclusion was, that one of their number must go and tell Walter and Mary, while the other two watched the body. It required quite as much courage as wisdom to reach this conclusion; for to tell the parents was a task the boys dreaded.

The lot was cast, country-boy fashion, with three blades of grass, to determine who should be the messenger of evil tidings. The lot fell upon Phil, and he immediately rose up to start. Ed suggested at this point, that, in sending word, the death ought to be ascribed to some cause. The boys had been very much puzzled from the first to know what *could* have done it. They gazed about the pasture-ground to discover what suggestion could be made. There were a couple of horses, some cows, and some sheep grazing in a distant part of the enclosure. As soon as it was suggested that one of the horses might perhaps have done it by kicking Willie, the boys accepted that as the natural and undoubted solution of the mystery. And so Phil took that word with him.

Phil went upon a little trot through the lot, and down the bank, moving rapidly, so that his heart might not have time to quail or shrink; and in less than five minutes he stood by the little house near the pond.

He looked in at the door, which was wide open upon this warm summer day, and there he saw Walter and Mary. Walter sat cleaning the lock of his rifle, while the gun itself was lying across his lap. Doubtless Phil's face was somewhat pale as he went in at the door; for

Mary looked at him as if she saw something there, and dreaded it.

The lad had good sense. He did not blurt out the sad news suddenly. He said to Walter, in a quiet way, "Will you please to step out of the door with me? I wish to see you."

It was the earnestness of the voice, perhaps, that caused the man to put aside his gun, and obey so quickly.

When they were out of the house, Phil said, "I have bad news for you. We have found your little son in the lot, kicked by a horse; and we are afraid that he is so bad that he is dead."

Phil had thought of this way of saying it before he got to the house. When he said dead, Walter gave a little start, and said, "Is he *dead?*"

Phil had to say, "Yes: we are afraid he is, and we *think* he is."

Walter stepped into the cottage, and Phil stood at the door, to see how he would tell Mary. Walter said, without any preface, "Mary, our little Willie is dead!"

"That was not a prudent thing," the boy thought, as the tragic words fell upon his ear, and fixed themselves in his memory.

The effects of the words upon Mary reminded the boy of the way he had seen a rifle-shot tell upon a rabbit or partridge. The woman passed through a kind of flutter or shudder for a moment, and then sunk straight down in a little heap upon the floor. Then followed a series of quick gasps, and catching for breath, and short exclamations of "Oh, dear! oh, dear!" and then the stifled shrieking began.

Walter took his wife up in his strong arms, and tried to undo in part the sad work which had been accomplished upon her by the few words he had so suddenly and imprudently uttered. He said that Willie might not be dead, after all, but only hurt. And so he placed her upon a bed; and he and Phil left her there, and started to go and see Willie.

Not many words were said as the man and boy climbed the bank, and strode hastily along to the fatal spot. As they neared it, there sat the two watchers, faithful to their post, and as still as statues.

Phil and Walter turned the angle of the fence, and the father came up to the body of his little son. He had not seemed stricken with grief until now, but only excited. As he looked steadily upon the chubby little form, all battered and bloody and bruised, the lad who had brought him there felt that some word must be said.

"It's a kick, ain't it?" said he.

This was hardly the right thing to say at such a moment, perhaps. The poor father choked and trembled, and replied, "A kick, or a bite, or something—oh, dear!" And then he turned his head and looked away, and there was the sound of his sobbing, and a strange, moaning cry.

Walter would not stay by the body, but directed the boys to remain and watch while he himself went and brought his friend the doctor. And then he turned away, and went off over the fields toward the settlement, uttering loud sobs, and that same strange cry.

It was hardly more than ten minutes' walk down to the road toward which Walter directed his steps; and in a very short time the boys saw groups of men coming from the houses, up the acclivity toward the fatal spot. They came hastily, two and three together; and soon a dozen or more were gathered around the three boys who had watched, and were gazing at the body.

After the first look, the men made characteristic remarks.

"That *is* a rough piece of business," said Dan.

"Fearful!" said Pete.

"That's durn queer work for a hoss, now, ain't it?" said Levi, a tall, keen fellow, intended by nature for a lawyer.

"It don't look like a hoss to me," said another.

And so they went on to comment and examine. It appeared that the rail under which Willie was jammed was dented and marked, as if hammered by many blows. The three innocent boys who had originated the "hoss theory," as the men called it, accounted for the marks on the rail by saying that the horse pawed at Willie after he was under the fence.

The men said they knew better. They began to question the boys, as if they entertained suspicions in regard to them; and the boys became very uncomfortable. The men asked repeatedly just how the body was lying when the boys had found it, and inquired again and again whether they had moved it at all. The lads felt these insinuations very keenly.

Men continued to come; and at length women came in groups, until quite an assembly was gathered there in the open field. Finally Walter returned slowly up the hill with a few friends, as if he were reluctant to come again to the place. Just as he reached the spot, good old father Moseley and his wife, a sharp, managing woman, came from the opposite direction, and met Walter. Father and mother Moseley lived down by the schoolhouse at the other side of the settlement.

Mother Moseley at once seized hold of Walter, and, while she wrung his hand, exclaimed in a high voice, that seemed to the boys not a becoming or natural voice in which to express grief,—

"O Walter! we can't give him up. No, no, no! Oh, dear!"

The gesticulation which accompanied this was tragic and stagey, and it was by far the most theatrical thing done upon that occasion.

Father Moseley spoke a few words which interested the people very much. Hearing some allusion made to the "hoss theory", he said,—

"The little boy down at the school says it was a sheep that did it."

And then it came out that Willie's playmate, Charlie Sanders, was "the little boy down at the school," and that Charlie had cried all the forenoon, and dared not tell the teacher what the matter was; but finally, at the noon-spell, he told a little girl that Willie did not come to school because a sheep in the lot had chased them, and knocked Willie down, and he could not get up.

Here was light indeed, especially for the three lads, who had begun to feel, since the horse theory was criticized, as if they themselves were culprits unless they accounted for "the murder."

Across the lot the sheep were still feeding. A young farmer stepped out of the crowd, and called "Nan, Nan, Nan!" and the flock, raising their heads, responded with a multitude of ba-a-s, and came galloping over the grassy field. At their head was "the old ram," a fine "buck," with great horns curling in spirals around his ears.

The young farmer held Willie's basket in one hand, and, making a brawny fist of the other, struck out toward the ram, offering him battle. The buck at once brought his head down in line of attack, squared himself for a big butt, and came on with a little run, and a charge, that, in an artistic point of view, was quite beautiful. The farmer, stepping aside, caught him by his horns as he came, and that magnificent charge was his last.

There was a bloodthirsty feeling pervading the crowd, undoubtedly; but Buck had a fair trial. There, on his white bold face and horns, were the bright carmine drops of fresh blood. No other witnesses were needed. In a moment a glittering keen knife flashed from some-

Willie 23

body's keeping into the bright sunshine, and in a moment more a purple stream dyed the white wool around Buck's throat, and there was a red pool upon the grass, and a little later, as Dan remarked, "some tough mutton."

The excitement abated; for the mystery was cleared up, and justice had its due. Kind-hearted Joe, who superintended the sabbath school, and led the religious element of the neighborhood, stepped forward, and said to the crowd,—

"Well, boys, it is all right here, and no suspicion, and no need of any ceremony. Let us take him home."

And then Joe took Willie in his arms, and held him closely, with the little face against his own, as if he were still living, and started for the cottage. Some of the people followed in a picturesque procession, through the pasture-lot, and down the bank, and along by the shore of the pond. When Walter's house was reached, a few of the women went in to soothe Mary; and Joe and the doctor went in also, and the people clustered about the door.

In the course of an hour it seemed that all had been done that could be done for Walter and Mary; and the people, except a few who remained as watchers and helpers, dispersed to their homes.

The three days that followed were bright, sunny days. A strange stillness and unusual hush reigned in the neighborhood of the cottage. The harsh, grating sound of the saw-mill was not heard as at other times;

for the mill was stopped in token of respect for the great sorrow. Only the softly flowing stream was heard, mingling its *susurrus* with the hum of the bees in the garden.

Now and then groups of children, dressed in their Sunday attire, would come down the bank, and, with hushed voices and fearful looks, steal up toward the cottage-door. Then kind Joe would see them, and would come out and take them in to see Willie; and after a few moments they would issue forth again, and walk sadly homeward; and, as they went, the sunlight dried their tears.

And farmers and hunters came from many miles away "to see the little boy that was killed by a sheep." Some of the rough men manifested their sympathy by exhibiting vindictive feelings toward the ram. After going in, and viewing the bruised corpse, they would come out with dark, determined looks, and grasping again the long rifles which they had brought with them, and "stood up" by the door, they would inquire of any bystander, with fierce emphasis, whether the ram that "did that" was dead. On being informed of his execution, they would say, *"That will do,"* with an air that implied how much they would have enjoyed it to have had a shot at him. Indeed, it appeared that if the poor brute had been possessed of fifty or a hundred lives, so that each irate hunter might have taken one, it would have been a great relief and satisfaction.

On the fourth day Willie was buried. Mary continued inconsolable. All of the social influences which the neighborhood could command were put in operation from the time of the funeral onward, in order to cheer her, and bind up her wounded spirit. Social meetings were held, and pleasant little gatherings made for her. Wherever there was enjoyment, Mary must be. She gratefully submitted herself to all their kindness, and tried to please her friends. But it seemed to do her little good. She remained pale, weak, and dispirited.

After a few months, Walter and Mary discovered that somehow they were not suited with their farm. They sold the place at the first opportunity, and returned to their former home in New England, the remains of little Willie having been forwarded in advance to a cemetery there, with which they in their early days had been familiar.

Ike's Wife

She was a subdued, sad-faced English woman, with deep-set, mournful eyes. I do not know what chance had brought her to the Adirondack Wilderness, or under what circumstances she had married Ike. He was an industrious laborer in the lumber-woods. Their dwelling was a log cabin in a little clearing near the edge of the forest.

Three men, returning home late in the evening from Whiskey Hollow, were walking along a path under the spruce and hemlock trees near Ike's cabin. Their names were Dan, Sandy, and Joe. It was very dark in the thick, leafy coverts. Joe carried a lantern, which formed a blur of light in the damp blackness under the evergreen forest. He looked at his watch by the light of the lantern, and told his comrades that it was ten o'clock.

Just then, as they were walking, there came what seemed a weak, distant cry through the darkness, and they stopped to listen. There was a low sound of the raindrops upon the leaves. The cry came again,—a faint shriek piercing the throbbing murmur of the falling rain.

Ike's Wife

It seemed to be the voice of a child.

"It must be over to Ike's," said Joe, reflecting soberly. "But," he added, "there is no child at Ike's."

"Yes, there is," said Dan: "they have adopted one lately."

"I think there is some trouble here," said Joe. "Come on, boys!" And then he impulsively left the path, and led the way with the lantern, his comrades following. Five minutes of floundering over fallen timber, and through the wet underbrush, brought them to the edge of Ike's little clearing. The cries had ceased as they reached the place. The men discovered a pale yellow bar of light thrust out through the one small window of the cabin, dimly revealing the misty drizzle, and the opaque darkness of the night.

The cries began again. The men walked hastily forward.

"Better rush in?" said Sandy inquiringly.

"No," said Joe: "I will knock at the door."

And he stood a moment, and listened. The sounds of blows and the shrieks of a child came out through the crevices of the log house.

"I can't stand this," said Joe nervously, and, stepping forward, he rapped loudly upon the door. There was no answer, and the cries continued. He grasped the latch-string with a jerk, and gave the door a push. It flew open, revealing the interior of the cabin, lighted by an open fire and lamplight. In the middle of the floor stood Ike's wife, with a stick in her hand, whipping a little girl apparently about eight years of age. The woman's face was pale, and her dark eyes gleamed. The child's back was partially bare, and blood was trickling down upon her flesh. The woman was so intent upon her cruel work, that she did not seem to notice the opening of the door. She brought the stick down twice more upon the little girl before Joe got to her, and seized her by the wrists, and said, "Why Lucy, what are you doing? Are you trying to kill the child?"

Ike's wife attempted no justification. She seemed to be roused as if from a dream. She sank down crying and sobbing, upon the floor. To the reproaches of the men she made no answer, except to wish that she was dead, and to say that she knew the Lord would never forgive her for being so angry with a child.

Joe turned, and soothed the little girl as well as he could, and examined her injuries, seeming greatly shocked by the marks upon her back. She was a spirited little person; and encouraged by the sympathy of the men, she denounced Ike's wife, her little chin quivering, and angry tears gathering in her eyes. After she was quieted, she informed the men that her name was Susie Murphy; that her "*own* mother" lived two miles away, and had a large family; and that Ike and his wife, having no children of their own, had adopted her as their little girl two months before; and that she "did not like it, and wanted to go home, please."

The men said, yes, perhaps she ought to go home; and Joe added, with a good deal of feeling, that there could be no excuse for such treatment of a child. He told Lucy that this was a curious and rather rough piece of work, she must admit; and he hoped no offence, but it must be "considered more or less." Lucy told the men to do whatever they thought best. They concluded to bring the mother of the child. Joe started out with his lantern, and, through the night and darkness, brought the Irish woman, who walked the two miles.

It was nearly an hour past midnight when the "own mother" reached the cabin, and saw her little girl.

She found words as well as tears to express her grief and indignation. Soft words for her "baby," and a hurricane of hard words for "the murtherin ould wolfe," were followed by a torrent of tears, after which came an attack upon Lucy with the fire-shovel, which was with difficulty restrained by the men.

The "own mother" insisted upon having the child taken home immediately. The little girl was therefore carefully wrapped up, and conveyed to her mother's cabin.

News of the affair spread rapidly. In the quiet atmosphere of the backwoods this was an exceedingly refreshing item. Every exaggeration that could increase the excitement, or bear against Lucy, was indulged in. At Whiskey Hollow it was currently reported that Ike Johnson's wife had "punished a helpless infant to that degree, by wallopin' it," that it was substantially flayed alive. It was further stated, "on good authority, though yer wouldn't believe it of a human woman, indeed yer wouldn't," that Ike's wife had whipped Susie regularly three times a day, except Sunday; and that she allowed her to sleep upon the door-mat; and that she kept her habitually in the dark passage called the cellar-way, and told her to watch for mice, letting her out at meal-times, and permitting her to crawl under the table, and kiss the toe of her mistress' shoe, and bark like a dog, and mew like a cat, for such food as was thrown to her. And these grim falsehoods were eagerly accepted as the exact truth of the case in Smith's barroom at the Hollow. And from this fountain, streams of information, flavored with whiskey, radiated to homes in the settlements and in the wilderness. This process of manufacturing and disseminating news increased the excitement from day to day.

Several of the men walked from the Hollow, a distance of three miles, to visit the little martyr, and, upon their return, expressed themselves as having seen a much more dreadful thing than they had expected. If any one who had not been, ventured to say a kind word for Lucy, the only answer was, "Wait until you have seen the child." Even good Deacon Jones, an office-bearer in the little church to which Lucy belonged, said with tragic feeling, "Wait until you have seen the child!"

All things considered, Whiskey Hollow and its environment enjoyed this sensation wonderfully. It furnished material for talk, and the theme was dwelt upon and exhausted in every aspect. The perils of female barrenness, and its tendency to change the disposition of "human wimin" into the ferocity of panthers, hyenas, and catamounts, was philosophized upon at great length by the soakers at the Hollow.

On the eleventh day after the whipping, Lucy was brought before a justice of the peace at the Hollow. The justice's office was crowded, and there was a multitude of people outside,—all eager to see the dreadful woman, as they termed poor, frightened Lucy.

Mrs. Murphy had Susie there on exhibition, and she excited a great deal of sympathy. Although but ten days had elapsed since the whipping, the healthy little Irish girl was so nearly healed of her wounds, that the mother found it necessary to coddle her a great deal, and to resort to many little artifices, to keep her appearing sufficiently miserable to answer the expectations of the public. At the first appearance of Lucy, Mrs. Murphy rushed forward to make an attack upon her. She was restrained from violent demonstrations; but her spirit was warmly commended by the people. Some of the men also shook their fists at Lucy openly, and were not reprimanded.

The justice's office was over the store. Ike and the constable helped Lucy, who was fearful and trembling, through the crowd, and up the stairs to the office. The prisoner was permitted to sit down upon a chair by the justice's desk.

The atmosphere of the crowded room was warm and stifling, and reeking with the fumes of bad whiskey and tobacco. Lucy sat a few moments, and then, before the proceedings commenced, became sick and very pale, and began to moan and quiver and cry. Ike tried to comfort her, but could not. She sunk down in a faint or swoon. A physician was sent for. In the mean time Lucy was placed upon a bench, and plied with simple restoratives.

"Is she playin' possum, think?" whispered Sandy Davenport of a friendly soaker at the door.

"No possum about that!" said the justice sharply as he overheard the inquiry.

In a few moments Lucy revived; and, being so placed as to get fresh air from a window, she remained conscious until the doctor came. He at once announced that his patient was so much depressed, and so seriously ill, that she could not with safety be detained by the justice.

The justice said that there must, of course, then be an adjournment. This announcement was received with expressions of dissatisfaction on the part of the crowd. The justice sternly commanded silence. There was a hush, and then a stifled murmur. Pete's whispered declaration that it was mighty queer law to let a critter that could mas-a-kree an infant in that way off on the score of delicate nerves, was generally approved. But the justice was firm and resolute. He adjourned the proceedings for twenty days.

A good deal of swearing was heard, and some jeering, as Lucy, half fainting with terror, was helped down the stairs, and into the wagon again. But there was no offer of violence.

Ike took his wife home. There she was left to brood in solitude, and struggle with dejection. Ike was compelled to be often absent at the lumber-camps and the mill. It was very gloomy: there were leaden November skies, and floods, and whirling snowflakes, and the winds ever moaning and sighing. Lucy, morbidly penitent, shrank and wept and shivered alone. Her church neglected her, and she felt that she was forsaken by the children of God. She told Ike that she had tried to look upward; but dreadful thoughts came between her soul and Him who loved the little ones. Even Infinite Pity, she said, turned away from one who could be cruel to a child. A sickening fear of the hour when she must again face the execrations of the people and the majesty of the law terrified and oppressed her. The physician said that she gained no rest except the brief sleep which his prescriptions procured. She told him once, that, with troubled dreams, she had also dreamed of home and the Christmas holidays in England. It was a cheerless waking to the dreadful thoughts and the rough cabin, with its one small window and the gloom and the cold. Only the blank silence was with her when Ike was away. No friendly footstep crossed her threshold in all the dreary days.

While Lucy was thus suffering and lonely, there was a great deal of speculation at Whiskey Hollow as to whether her nervousness was real, or a dodge to escape justice. The strife ran so high upon this question, that not only Lucy's sincerity, but the honesty of the magistrate and the physician were arraigned. Some decisive action was longed for.

The characteristic plan of executing that just judgement, which, it was argued, the law denied, was resolved upon. A committee of five "most respected citizens," selected in the bar-room, accepted the appointment, and said they would "do it." It was a semi-secret arrangement, and there was a claim of entire fairness in it. Nothing would be done, if, at the expiration of the twenty days, Lucy should appear, and be "put through according to law."

But the twenty days expired, and, by the advice of the physician, Lucy did not appear, and there was a further postponement; and the committee resolved to do their work.

"She shall be treated entirely respectful," said Pete, the leader at the bar-room; "but blood must be drawn, and justice honored, in these ere parts."

There came a clear autumn evening. Ike was known to be away at the lumber-camp. At nightfall the five men sallied forth upon their lawless errand.

Craunch, craunch, craunch, sounded the footsteps of the party upon the thin, crispy snow, as, emerging from the gloom of the woods into the open clearing they marched in single file up in front of Ike's cabin. The house was dark, and no sound issued from it. The men gathered in a group in front of the door, and listened. It was a very bright night: the full moon was sailing in the burnished sky overhead. Only the voice of the creek singing below relieved the stillness of the forest.

"Is she playin' possum, think?" said Sandy in a whisper.

Ike's Wife

"Heerd us comin', maybe," said Sol Davis.

Pete stepped to the door, and gave the latchstring a jerk, and the door a push. The door seemed to hit against some obstacle, and then slip by it: another push, and it was wide open. The white moonlight streamed in, and fell upon a dark, shadowy something which was swinging, like a huge pendulum, to and fro from the impulse the door had given it. As it swung in and out of the moonlight, the men saw the feet of a woman and her trailing skirts. It was Lucy, dead, hanging by a rope from a rafter of the cabin, the light of her sweet life quenched in the awful night of insanity and self-destruction.

The lawless group stood aghast, and so still, that the swinge of the rope chafing against the timber could be distinctly heard.

The silence continued for what seemed a very long time. It was finally broken by Pete, who said in a suppressed voice, "My God! she has hung herself!"

The next impulse and suggestion was to close the door, and steal silently away from the place.

A little discussion rendered it clear that such a course could not be pursued. "There is no use of skulking," said Sol Davis. "They know we come here: we must make the best of this ere, and be neighborly."

Matches and birch-bark were produced, and in a few moments the ruddy flame of a camp-fire reddened the snowy landscape in front of the cabin. As the flame leaped up, a startled owl in a dark spruce-top at the edge of the clearing uttered a thrilling scream of surprise, and fluttered away into the gloom of the forest.

The party took counsel one with another, and decided that the news should be immediately spread abroad. Two of the men, therefore, went to Whiskey Hollow to carry the intelligence, while the others remained and watched. Before midnight about thirty men and boys had come to the place, and stood around the camp-fire in the little clearing.

It was resolved to explore the interior of the cabin. This was speedily done with the aid of bark-torches. A clock, fixed upon a rude shelf, was found to be nibbling the minutes away as usual, and the ashes upon the hearth were still warm. It was apparent that Lucy had not been very long dead. Her appearance and the surrounding objects were carefully scrutinized. She was neatly and even tastefully dressed, as if for some special and public occasion. The white, shrunken face, in its mute, appealing sorrow, touched the hearts of the rough men, as they removed the corpse, and placed it upon the one bed in the cabin. A letter in Lucy's handwriting was found open upon the table. It revealed her tender love for her husband, and her sense of the great crime which she thought she had committed. It set forth the idea, existing in her own distempered imagination, that her life was the only expiation that could atone for offending one of His little ones. She expressed the hope that the sacrifice she made would show the sincerity of her repentance, and be accepted by the great Head of the church and by the people. At the close of the letter, she begged Ike to present her clothing, and all the little treasures she had, to "dear Susie."

As one of the men slowly spelled out the words of this letter by the firelight in front of the cabin, the others, in a close huddle around him, listened with rapt attention. When it came to the closing words about Susie, there was a deeper hush; and, after the reading had ceased, the men were silent.

Finally one said, "I do not say but we did wrong by Lucy, boys."

"She was a real woman, arter all; hey, boys?" snuffled Sandy, his eyes moistening with the ready tearfulness of one who is habitually steeped in whiskey.

Pete said, with an attempt at frankness in his manner, "They ought to 'a come here—some of the women had. They no business to let her worry herself to death all alone in this way. And what right had Ike to leave her so, I'd like to know."

And so this group of men from Whiskey Hollow, by the firelight looked in each other's faces, and felt that they were innocent, as, with happy ingenuity, they rolled the burden from their own shoulders on to Ike and the women.

The news of Lucy's death by her own hand shocked the backwoods community. There was a great deal of gossip in regard to it; and some regret was expressed for the cruel neglect from which she had suffered.

Two days after the discovery of the death, the funeral took place from Ike's cabin. It was on a bright Sunday afternoon of clear sunshine. A thin ribbon of smoke from the dying camp-fire curled gracefully up in the still air. About fifty men and women were in and around the cabin in their rough backwoods dress. Ike sat outside with the men, upon a log, by the smouldering embers.

Brother Gaston, an exhorter, conducted the religious exercises. After reading the Scriptures, prayer, and exhortation, he said, "Our bereaved brother here wishes to make a few remarks."

Ike did not rise up from his seat on the log, but cleared his throat, and, with some long pauses caused by natural feelings, said, "I always stand by them that are mine. Friends and neighbors, I just wanted to say that my Lucy here was a good girl. She was used to a better home than here in the woods. And it wa'n't my Lucy her own self that did this that has happened. Two years ago she was sick and poorly, and the doctor give her opium for a long time. It appears as if she got so she could not live without it. Well, the doctor told me I must keep it from her, and I did; but it made her about crazy. Of course I do not stand up for the way she whipped the child, although it was a most uncommon provokin' child, I must say. But it wa'n't my Lucy that did it. I say it was the opium,—when she didn't have it, and couldn't get it, of course. And likewise it was the opium that killed her. Lucy was a good girl, and a good true wife to me."

The muscles around Ike's mouth began to quiver, and he broke down, sobbing with great grief. Sandy went up to him, and sat down upon the log beside him, and, putting his arm around the mourner, spoke low words of sympathy and consolation. Some of the women wept. An aged matron, standing in the doorway of the cabin, said, "My brethren and sisters, she that lies here was good and truthful. I would that I had died as young and innocent as she was! This lonely place had no rest for her."

"Let us sing a hymn," said brother Gaston; and he struck up the mournful tune called China. The melody rose and fell in long-drawn cadences like the wailing voice of the forest-trees. The women chimed in with a shrill treble, and the wild jays in the treetops answered in ringing falsetto notes.

When the singing had ceased, the procession formed, and proceeded out of the clearing, along the path through the woods, towards a burying-place by the creek.

As the men filed along, two and two, under the trees, many kind words were said in memory of Lucy, and many expressions of sincere sorrow were uttered for her untimely and melancholy death. Upon a sandy knoll, where brier-bushes grew, and where the wild birds sang, and the music of the flowing creek was near, they buried Ike's wife.

John's Trial

Just where the Wilderness road of the Adirondack Highlands strikes the edge of the great Champlain Valley, in a little clearing, is a lonely log house. On the tenth day of July, 1852, a muscular, gaunt woman stood at the door of the house, overlooking the vast extent of the valley. From her stand-point, ten miles of green forest swept down to the lake's winding shore. She saw the indentation made in the shore line by "the bay," and beyond, the wide waters gleaming in the fervid brightness of summer. Specks were here and there discernible in the light, flashed back from the blue, mirror-like surface, and by long watching it could be seen that these specks were moving to and fro.

The woman knew that these distant moving atoms were boats freighting lumber through Lake Champlain. She knew there was but one boat that would be likely to turn aside, and come into the little bay, and that this boat would be her son John's sloop.

That was why she watched so anxiously a speck that neared the bay, and at length entered it. To make doubly sure, she brought to bear an old spyglass, whose

John's Trial

principal lens was cracked entirely through. It gave her a smoky view of the famous sloop, "The Dolly Ann," John's property; and then she was entirely certain that her son, who had been three weeks absent on his voyage, was coming home.

Jupiter the house-dog, who had been watching her, seemed to know it too, perfectly well; for, as she turned from her survey through the glass, his canine nature developed a degree of wriggling friskiness of which the grave old dog seemed half ashamed. He whined, and walked about the door-yard for a few moments, then gave his mistress a long, steady look, and, seeming satisfied with what he read in her face, jumped over the fence, and started down the road into the valley, at a full-run.

The woman knew that three or four hours must yet elapse before John and Jupiter would come along the path together, tired by their long tramp up the mountain-side. She thought and waited, as lonely mothers think and wait for absent sons.

At about four o'clock a young, dark-eyed man and the dog came up the road and to the house. "Heigho, mother, all well?" was the man's greeting. The woman's greeting was only, "How do you do, John?" There was no show of sentiment, not even a hand-shake; but a bright look in the man's face, and a tremor in the voice of the woman, conveyed the impression that these plain people felt a great deal more than they expressed.

Two hours passed away; and, after supper, the neighbors, who had seen John and the dog come up the road, dropped in for a talk with "the captain," as John was called by his friends.

Soon the inquiry was made, "Where did you leave your cousin William?"

John had taken his cousin William, who lived upon the lake-shore, with him upon this last trip, and hence the question.

But John did not answer the question directly. He seemed troubled and unhappy about it. He finally acknowledged that he and William had not agreed, and that high words and blows had passed between them, and added that his cousin had finally left the boat, and had gone away in a huff, he knew not where, but somewhere into the pineries of Canada. He declared, getting warm in his recollection of the quarrel, that he "didn't care a darn" where Will went, anyway.

A month passed away: it was August. Cousin Will did not return. But certain strange stories came up the lake from Canada, and reached the dwellers along the Adirondack Wilderness road. No cousin William had been seen in the pineries; but just across the Canada line, at the mouth of Fish River, where the sloops were moored to receive their lading of lumber, a bruised, swollen, festering corpse had risen, and floated in the glare of a hot, August day. The boatmen rescued it, and buried it upon the shore. They described it as the body of a hale, vigorous young man, agreeing in height, size, and appearance with cousin William.

And there was another story told by the captain of a sloop which had been moored at the mouth of Fish River, near by John's sloop, on the fatal voyage from which cousin William had not returned.

The captain said, that, upon the 4th of July, he had heard quarrelling upon John's sloop all the afternoon, and had noticed that only two men were there. He thought the men had been drinking. At nightfall there was a little lull; but soon after dark the noise broke out again. He could see nothing through the gloom; but he heard high and angry words, and at length blows, and then a dull, crushing thud, followed by a plunge into the water; and then there was entire silence. He listened for an hour, in the stillness of the summer night, but heard no further sound from the boat. In the early gray of the next morning, the captain, looking across the intervening space to John's sloop, which he described as hardly a stone's-throw from his own, saw a hat lying upon the deck, and, using his glass, was confident that he saw "spatters of blood." He thought it "none of his business," and, taking advantage of a light breeze, sailed away, and said nothing. But, when the floating corpse was found, he felt sure there had been a murder, and, as he expressed it, felt bound to tell his story like an honest man, and so told it.

Putting these things together, it soon grew to be the current opinion upon the lake, that Capt. John had murdered his cousin William. The dwellers upon the Wilderness road also came, by slow degrees, and unwillingly, to the same conclusion. It was felt and said that John ought to be arrested.

Accordingly, on a dreary day in November, two officers from the county town, twenty miles away down the lake-shore, came and climbed the steep road to the lonely log house, and arrested John. It was undoubtedly a dreadful blow to those two lonely people living isolated in the wilderness. Perhaps there ought to have been some crying and a scene; but there was no such thing. The officers testified that neither John nor his mother made any fuss about it. There was a slight twitching of the strong muscles of her face as she talked with the officers, but no other outward sign.

John gave more evidence of the wound he felt. He was white and quivering; yet he silently, and without objection, made ready to go with the officers. He was soon prepared, and they started. John, as he went out of the door, turned and said, "Good-by: it will all be made right, mother." She simply answered, "Yes, good-by: I know it, my son."

The trio went on foot down the road to the next house, where the officers had left their team. Jupiter, standing up with his fore-paws upon the top of the fence, gazed wistfully after them. When they passed around the bend of the road, out of sight, Jupiter went into the house. The strong woman was there about her work, as usual; but the heavy tears would now and then fall upon the hard pine floor. She knew that her own boy would spend the coming night in the county jail.

John's Trial

At twelve o'clock of that chill November night, the woman and the dog went out of the house: she fastened the door, and then they went together down the dark mountain-road, while the autumn winds swept dismally through the great wilderness, and the midnight voice of the pines mourned the dying year. The next day, at noon, a very weary woman on foot, with a small bundle and a large dog, put up at the little village hotel hard by the county jail.

Another day passed, and then the preliminary examination came on before a justice, to determine whether there was sufficient evidence to hold John in custody until a grand jury of the county should be assembled for the next Court of Oyer and Terminer.

Three days were spent in this examination before the justice; the captain of the sloop who had overheard the quarrel in the night told his story, and the boatmen who had found the body told theirs. Two men who had been the crew of John's little vessel were also called; but they could tell little more than that they were absent on shore upon the 4th of July, and when they returned to the vessel, William had gone, they knew not where nor why.

The evidence against John seemed to the magistrate clear and conclusive. But the counsel for the accused (employed by John's mother) took the ground, that, as the offence was committed in Canada, a justice in the United States had no jurisdiction in the matter.

This view prevailed, and after five days the accused

was set at liberty. But that voice of the people, which the ancient proverb says is like the voice of God, had decided that John was guilty. It was under this crushing comdemnation that John and his mother left the county town on a cold December day, turning their steps homeward; and at evening they climbed the acclivity so familiar to them, and reached the lonely log house upon the mountain. Their neighbors were glad to see them back again, but were plain to say that "it appeared like as if John was guilty." These dwellers in the solitudes were accustomed to speak truly what they thought. John and his mother, too, spoke openly of this matter. It was only of showing affection and love that these people were ashamed and shy. They both admitted to their neighbors that the evidence was very strong; but John added quietly that he was not guilty, as if that settled the whole matter.

But the voice of the people, and a sense of justice, would not let this crime rest. It came to be very generally known that a man guilty of murder was living near the shore of Lake Champlain unmolested. Arrangements were effected by which it came to pass that Canadian authorities made a formal application to the the United States for the delivery of one John Wilson, believed to be guilty of the murder of his cousin William Wilson.

And so again two officers, this time United States officials, climbed up to the little log house upon the edge of the great valley. Through a drifting, blinding storm of snow they were piloted by a neighbor to the lonely house. They made known their errand; and, in the course of half an hour, the officers and their prisoner were out in the storm en route for the distant city of Montreal.

It was many days before the woman saw her son again. For four months John was imprisoned, awaiting his trial before the Canadian courts. Doubtless those four months seemed long to the solitary woman. She had not much opportunity to indulge in melancholy fancies: she spent much of her time in pulling brush and wood out of the snow, and breaking it up with an axe, so as to adapt it to the size of her stove.

The neighbors tried to be kind, and often took commissions from her to the store and the gristmill in the valley. "But after all," said Pete Searles, one of John's friends, in speaking of the matter afterward, "what could neighbors amount to, when the nearest of them lived a mile away, and all of them plain to say that they believed she was the mother of a murderer?"

But the neighbors said the woman did not seem to mind the solitude and the rough work. Morning, noon, and night she was out in the snow or the storm at the little hovel of a barn back of the house, taking care of two cows and a few sheep which were hers and John's. At other times travellers upon the Wilderness road would see her gaunt, angular figure clambering down a rocky ridge, dragging poles to the house to be cut up for fuel.

She received two letters from John in the course of

the winter. The first told her that he was imprisoned, and awaiting his trial in Montreal; and the next one said that his trial had been set down for an early day in March.

This correspondence was all the information the mother had of her son; for the lake was frozen during the winter, so that the boats did not run, and no news could come from Canada by the boatmen.

When March came and passed away without intelligence from John, it was taken by the dwellers upon the lake-shore and along the wilderness road as a sure indication that he had been convicted of the crime. A letter or newspaper announcing the fact was confidently looked for by the neighbors whenever they went to the distant post-office for their weekly mail.

As March went out, and spring days and sunshine came, it was noticed that the face of John's mother looked sharp and white; but she went about the same daily duties as before, without seeming to feel ill or weak.

On a plashy April day full of sunshine, she stood on the rocky ridge back of the house, looking down upon the lake. A few early birds had come back, and were twittering about the clearing. Although the snow still lingered in patches upon the highlands, the valley looked warm below, and the first boats of the season were dotting the wide, distant mirror of "old Champlain." A man came slowly up the muddy line of road, through the gate, and around the house; then first the woman saw him. A slight spasm passed over her face. There was a little pitiful quiver of the muscles about the mouth, and then she walked slowly down the ridge to where the man stood. She struggled a little with herself before she said, "Well, John, I am glad to see you back."

John tried to be cool also; but nature was too much for him. He could not raise his eyes to hers; and his simple response, "Yes, mother," was chokingly uttered.

The two walked into the house together in the old familiar way. The woman, without a word, began to spread the table; and her son went out and prepared fuel, and, bringing it in, replenished the fire. Then he sat down in his accustomed place by the stove, with a pleasant remark about how well the fire burned, and how good it seemed to be home again. And the woman spoke a few kind, motherly words.

It was the way they had always done when John came back; but now there was a great sadness in it, for he had come "*from prison.*" Jupiter seemed fully to realize the situation. He exhibited none of that friskiness which characterized the welcome he had usually given; but, when John was seated, the old dog came slowly up to him, laid his fore-paws and his head in his master's lap, and looked sadly in his face.

As they sat down to supper, John began to tell of his fare in the jail at Montreal, and to speak freely of his life there. "Will you have to go back?" said his mother, with that quiver about the mouth again. "No, mother," said John: "it is finished, and I am discharged."

After supper the story was told over, how well John's counsel had worked for him, and how the judge had said there was not sufficient evidence to convict of so great a crime.

John continued from this time on, through the spring, to live at home. He allowed his sloop to float idly in the bay, while, as he said, he himself rested. The truth was, he saw, as others did not, that his mother had carried a fearful weight, and now, when it was lifted by his return, that the resources of her life were exhausted. The change, not yet apparent to other eyes, was clear to his vision. So it is that these silent spirits read each other.

As the warm weather advanced, the strong woman became weak; and, as the June flowers began to bloom, she ceased to move about much, and sat the most of each day in a chair by the open door. John managed the house, and talked with his mother. Her mind changed with the relaxation of her physical frame. She no longer strove to hide her tears, but, like a tired infant, would weep, without restraint or concealment, as she told her son of the early loves and romance of her girlhood life in a warm valley of the West. He learned more of his mother's heart in those June days than he had surmised from all he had known of her before. And he understood what this predicted. He felt that the heart nearest his own was counting over the treasures of life ere it surrendered them forever.

There was no great scene when the woman died. It

was at evening, just as the July fervors were coming on. She had wept much in the morning. As the day grew warm she became very weak and faint, and about noon was moved by her son from her chair to her bed, and so died as the sun went down.

John was alone in the house when she died. Since his return from Montreal, he had been made to feel that he had but one friend besides his mother. Only one neighbor had called upon him, and that was Pete Searles. *He* had ever proved true. But John did not like to trouble his one friend, who lived two miles away, to come and stay with him during the night: so he lighted a candle, took down from a shelf a little Bible and hymn-book that he and his mother had carried on an average about four times a year to a schoolhouse used as a church, some six miles away; and so, alone with the dead, he spent the hours in reading and tears and meditation.

In the morning he locked the door of his home, and walked "over to Pete's." As he met his friend, he said in a clear voice, but with eyes averted, "She has gone, Pete. If you will just take the key and go over there, I'll go down to the lake, and get the things, and tell Downer, and we'll have the funeral, say on Thursday."

Pete hesitated a moment, then took the key John offered him, and said, "Yes, John: I will tell my woman, and we will go over and fix it, and be there when you come back." And so John went on his way. "Downer" was the minister, and "the things" were a coffin and a shroud.

On Thursday was the funeral. Pete took care to have all the people of the neighborhood there, although it hardly seemed as if John desired it. The popular voice, having once decided it, still held John as a murderer, and claimed that he was cleared from the charge only by the tricks of his lawyer. John knew of this decision. At the funeral he was stern, cold, white, and statue-like. While others wept, but few tears fell from his eyes; and even these seemed wrung from him by an anguish, for the most part suppressed or concealed.

He chose that his mother should be buried, not in the "burying-ground" at the settlement, but upon their own little farm where she had lived. And so, in a spot below the rocky ridge, where wild violets grew, she was laid to rest.

John spent the night following the funeral at Pete's house, then returned to his own home, and from that time his *solitary* life began. He took his cattle and his sheep over to Pete's, made all fast about his home, and resumed his boating upon Lake Champlain. He fully realized that he was a marked man. He was advised, it was said even by his own legal counsel, to leave the country, and to leave his name behind him; but no words influenced him. Firm and steady in his course, strictly temperate and just, he won respect where he could not gain confidence.

The years rolled by. Capt. John still was a boatman, and still kept his home at the lonely log house on the edge of the great valley. From each voyage he returned, and spent a day and night alone at the old place; and it was noticed that a strong, high paling was built around his mother's grave, and a marble head-stone was placed there, and other flowers grew with the wild violets. Even in winter, when there was no boating, and he boarded down by the lake, he made many visits to the old homestead. His figure, which, though youthful, was now growing gaunt and thin, as his mother's had been, was often seen by Pete at nightfall upon the top of a certain rocky ridge, standing out clear and sharp against the cold blue steel of the winter sky.

John had no companions, and sought none. The young men and women of his set had married and settled in life: he was still the same.

But there came a change. Eleven years had passed since the mother died, and it was June again. John was spending a day at the old place once more. He sat in the door, looking out on the magnificent landscape,—the broad lake, and the dim line of mountains away across the valley. The lovely day seemed to cheer this stern, lonely man.

Three persons came up the road: they advanced straight to where John was sitting. One of them stepped forward, looked John steadily in the face, held out his hand to him, and said, "John, do you know me?"

The voice seemed to strike him with a sharp, stunning shock. He quivered, held his breath, stared into the eyes of the questioner, and then, suddenly becoming unnaturally cool and collected, said, "Is it you, William?"

The two who stood back had once been John's warmest friends. They now came forward, and, with such words as they could command, told the story of William's sudden return, and sought for themselves forgiveness for the cruel and false suspicion which had so long estranged them from their friend.

John seemed to hear this as one in a dream. He talked with William and the men, in a manner that seemed strangely cold and indifferent, about where William had been voyaging so long in distant seas and of his strange absence. A quarter of an hour passed away. The men proposed that John should go with them to their homes, and said there would be a gathering of friends there. They pressed the invitation with warmth, and such true feeling as our voices express when a dear friend has been greatly wronged, and we humbly acknowledge it.

John said absently, in reply, that he did not know. He looked uneasily around as if in search of something,—perhaps his hat. He essayed to rise from his chair, but could not, and in a moment he fell back, ashy pale, fainting, and breathless. The men had not looked for this; but, accustomed as they were to the rough life of the wilderness, they were not alarmed. They fanned the fainting man with their straw hats, and, as soon as water could be found, applied it to his hands and face. He soon partially recovered, and looking up, said in a broken voice, "Give me a little time, boys." At this hint the two old friends, who were now crying, stepped out of the door, and cousin William sat down out upon the door-step.

John found that a *little* time was not enough. He had travelled too long and far in that fearful desert of loneliness easily or quickly to return. A nervous fever followed the shock he received, and for two months he did not leave the homestead, and was confined to his bed. But the old house was not lonely: the men and women came, both his old friends and some new-comers, and tried to make up to him in some degree the love and sympathy he had so long missed. But for many days it was evident that their kindness pained and oppressed him.

"It appears like," said Pete, "that a rough word don't hurt him; but a kind one he can't stand." And this was true. His soul was fortified against hatred and contempt; but a kind voice, or a gentle caress, seemed to wound him so that he would sob like an infant.

As he recovered from his illness, he continued gentle, kind, and shrinking to a fault. By the operation of some spiritual law that I do not fully comprehend, he was, after his recovery, one of those who win a strange affection from others. His influence seemed like a mild fascination. It was said of him in after-years that he was more truly loved, and by more people, than any other man or woman in all the settlements round. Children loved him with a passionate attachment, and the woman of childlike nature whom he made his wife is said to have died of grief at his death. He departed this life at the age of thirty-eight years; and he sleeps on the edge of the great valley, with his mother and his wife beside him.

An Adirondack Neighborhood

There was a freedom in the neighborhood that I have never found anywhere else. The mountains and a hundred miles of woods shut us out from the busy life of "the States." The vast dim landscape below to the northward was "only Canada." The isolation was considerable.

The neighborhood was not a small place: we knew literally everybody for a dozen miles around. It made it very much of a home indeed, and very pleasant, to have so wide an acquaintance, and to never meet strange faces. There was an utter lack of formality.

I am telling about the neighborhood as it was many years ago; but, so far as a mere description of the place is concerned, I might just as well tell how it is now. For the place does not change. It is as wild and free as ever. Only last summer, when I went home, my brothers and relatives who reside there, and the neighbors, were telling me all about the bear that had eaten the corn last fall, until the men caught him at it, and chased him across the lots, and down the road, and killed him. The women said they were all out looking at the sport, and one woman drove him away from her door-yard with a piece of a board. The accounts which were given of the transaction were as fresh and picturesque as the stories that used to thrill me when we first went there to live many years ago.

I will not turn aside to tell the story of the bear-chase; but I must allude to several graphic points made by the people in telling of it. A classification of dog-nature that was dwelt upon was amusing. It seemed that there were three kinds of dog made apparent in the chase. There was the wise and faithful hound, that hung to the bear, and nipped him when he tried to run, but kept out of his way when he turned to strike; there was the house-dog, who, when he came near, suddenly paused as he saw what it was, and turned with a resigned air, and ran swiftly into the house, and crawled under the bed, and remained there until the next morning; and there was the small yellow dog, that had no idea of a bear, but came right up to the brute as if it had been a domestic animal. According to the account, the yellow dog soared suddenly into the atmosphere, fell into the river some forty feet away, was fished out, and dried by the stove for an hour, after which he began to whimper, and recognize his friends. It seemed that the dogs remembered and understood the facts of the case. Old Sport, the hound, listened in my presence, to an account of the adroit manner in which he had tumbled the bear off a crossing-log into the river, with evident appreciation; while the yellow dog went away behind the house whenever any thing was said about the bear.

An Adirondack Neighborhood

A good deal was made of the fact that aunt Eri (Eri's wife) had first seen the tall black figure of Bruin across the lots, picking corn, and had thought it was the colportor, as nobody else in the neighborhood ever wore black; but, as the figure settled down upon all-fours, she made out what it was. The final heading-off of the animal right in the road, and his death, and the gathering of men, women, and children to see, were described in a way that I am not able to put into words. It needs the gestures. I can only say, that, with the usual freedom of the place, the men committed extravagances. They yelled, and hugged each other, and fired guns, and jumped upon the dead bear. One strong man lifted a huge bowlder, and jounced it down on the bear's head.

It was made a point that the men liked the bear-meat; but the women did not: and it was regarded as a joke by the men, that large sections of the flesh were furtively used by the housewives for soap-grease.

To return to the days of long-ago: we three brothers were boys, when our family moved into this neighborhood. The place and the people interested us very much. There were some queer characters. There was the man down the river who had heard of a run-away pond which destroyed a good deal of property, and who therefore lived in constant fear that the lake at the head of our river would get away, and come down upon us. He slept in the garret of his house, with a small boat hanging out of the window, ready for the emergency. There was also the nervous, timid man, who was always excited for three days after leaving his quiet home, and visiting "The Corners," and the store and the mill. Our nearest neighbor was a famous fisherman—in his own little brook; but he had never in all his life ventured into the deep woods. He astonished us by his almost superstitious respect for the wilderness. In all his younger days he had desired to visit the wonderful places in the famous South Woods, as men in other localities desire to visit Europe; but the cares of home had prevented him, until he had become too old to make the journey. He told us, in all confidence and good faith, that a far-off mountain, called Whiteface, was too precipitous for any human foot to climb. It was known, however, that the top was composed of silver-ore. That was what made it so white. The Indians knocked off pieces of the silver with their arrows. So he had understood, and he regarded it as a probable story.

The general tendency in the neighborhood was to exaggerate the marvels of the forest. It happened late one evening that our neighbor Ralph and his two daughters, returning home from a visit, saw by the light of their lantern a panther right in the road before them. As the light struck his face, the creature turned, and dashed off into the woods. It was a great scare to the little party, and produced a wonderful excitement in the neighborhood. The incident afforded opportunity to exaggerate, and some queer reminiscences were narrated. One story was, that a painter (so they called it) away off somewhere in the mountains, had jumped down from a

An Adirondack Neighborhood   61

tree, and seized a boy sixteen years old. The story ran that this pussy of the woods had taken the boy alive to the top of a lofty pine, there played with him as if he were a mouse, throwing him into the air in a lively manner, and catching him as he came down. The gradual weakening of the young man in the paws of the panther, until he became "limpsy," so that his agonized mother, who stood at the foot of the tree, gazing upward, and watching the operation, could see that her son was at last dead, was a very thrilling part of the grim recital. Preposterous as the story seemed, it was narrated, not to say trembled over, with an air of deep conviction by some of the story-tellers of the neighborhood.

Another incident will illustrate the feeling which existed, among those who were not hunters by occupation, in regard to the dangers of the forest. A sturdy neighbor went with a party into a very wild, unfrequented section to hunt and fish. He accidentally strayed away from his comrades. Finding himself alone, he began to run, and fire his gun. His comrades pursued him. It was difficult to catch him. He seemed wild or insane. He avoided his pursuers as if he had been a wild beast. When they caught him, he was very pale, and beside himself. And yet he was within a day's journey of his home; and following any water-course down the northward incline for ten or fifteen hours would have brought him to the cleared country.

There was, however, some excuse in this locality for regarding the wilderness with such profound consideration. Several persons had been lost in it, and some had perished. It required a journey of about a hundred miles through the long, narrow lane of arable land between the wilderness and Canada, and so around the mountains, to get fairly out of the shadow of the forest.

To us boys, who were new-comers, and had read much of the Adirondacks, the woods were full of interest. We passed many days in the trackless solitudes with only a pocket compass as guide. There is no other loneliness so deep and solemn, or that so haunts the imagination, and is so full of joy and fear to the boyish spirit, as the far-away loneliness that is felt in the gloomy, trackless wilderness. With a party, or upon well-known routes, this is not experienced. But it will be understood that this feeling of loneliness may be very strong in young and inexperienced persons, whose travels are to them adventurous explorations.

Some of our first adventures in the forest left a deep impression upon our minds. Jule, the eldest, was the first of our youthful trio who sought to gratify the curiosity we felt in reference to the deep woods. It was the summer of our arrival at our new home. It was in August. He went alone a day's journey into the forest, and camped a dozen miles away from even a hunter's cabin. He did not burden himself with a gun. His outfit consisted of some bread and butter, a pocket compass, and a bunch of matches. The only serious adventure he met with was in the night. It was merely a few sudden footsteps near him, and the whistle of a deer enlivening his reflections, as he sat nodding over his little fire of bark and dried branches. It should be added that he was a thorough sceptic in regard to the alleged dangers of the forest, and cared nothing for mere hunting and fishing. He was a lover of nature, and enthusiastic disciple of Wilson and Audubon.

I will endeavor to give an adequate and truthful idea of adventures in the Adirondack Wilderness, in that part of this wild region where we were located. I know of no way to do this so well as to sketch our own juvenile experience.

The trip that first suggests itself in this connection is one that was made very soon after Jule's solitary excursion. It was his excursion that gave rise to this second one a week later. I recall it the more vividly, because it was the only occasion upon which any of us were driven out of the woods. It had been resolved to reach, if possible, two lonely ponds called twin-lakes, said to be hidden between mountains, and not easily found. Two of our youthful trio started on this quest, and had made the best part of a day's journey into the forest wilds, when it began to rain. They undertook to camp; but suddenly there sprang up a sound of voices so unearthly and terrific, that it seemed to freeze the very marrow in their bones. In the deep stillness the sounds were fearful. A very sincere desire to get out of the woods as quickly as possible was felt and acted upon. A desperate rush was made. By the aid of the compass a water-course which led to the clearings was fortunately found. A good stretch was made before dark; and stumbling along through the night, home was reached before morning. It turned out that the awful voices which had been heard came from a pack of wolves howling in the lone dreariness of the rainy afternoon. One of the adventurers who retreated from this wild music was only fourteen years of age. Since that time he has seen life in the wilds of California, and among the Sierras, and has faced death upon the field of battle; but he still refers to that scare among the Adirondacks, when he was so young and so easily impressed, as his most thrilling experience.

Another excursion was made in September of the same year. The adventures of that excursion are, in my memory, among the freshest and brightest I have known of Adirondack life. A sketch of the main incidents that occurred will present a good specimen of the Adirondack woods as we found them.

The entire trio joined in the excursion this time. Ed, the youngest, was as eager for hunting and fishing as the ornithologist Jule was to observe the habits of rare birds, and to study nature. Phil was the connecting link between the other two.

It was not quite sunrise when the little party of three entered the dark spruce-forest, leaving home, and anxious parents and friends, and sympathizing neighbors, behind them. The woods in which the night-shadows still lingered, were at first very gloomy; but soon the sun shot his arrows through the thick boughs, and made it pleasant. For hours they followed a water-course. It was hard, steady, monotonous effort. Every eye and ear was intent; and the one small rifle was always ready. But those who know the woods need not be told that scarcely a sign of life appeared. Except the Canada jay and the woodpecker, the birds had been left behind at the clearing. At times the stillness was oppressive; at other times the shrill falsetto note of the jay, or the tap of the woodpecker, would relieve the silence. It was noticed that one other familiar friend was a dweller in the solitudes: here and there a red squirrel, away up in some lofty black-spruce top, would discover the party, and begin his tantalizing chickaree and nervous sputter, and continue it as long as they were in his neighborhood.

At about nine o'clock, after four hours' hard marching, Jule decided that the point had been reached at which it was proper to leave the water-course, and, inclining toward the left, take a south-easterly bearing in order to travel in a direction toward the twin-lakes. This was a matter of judgment only,—an inference from an estimate of the distance that had already been passed over. After looking up and down the water-course, and trying to fix upon some object that could be identified as the point of departure, a mass of rock beside a twisted tree was found, and from that point the departure was made. Then followed slow, monotonous, toilsome walking under the spruces and elm-trees and birches of the primeval forest. It was hard work fighting a way through the underbrush, and over the decayed and fallen logs. In that kind of journeying one tires, not the feet alone, but the entire frame. The hands are in almost constant use in climbing, and in pushing a way through the brush.

The compass was now the guide. The instrument, which was carried by Jule, was a little, cheap affair, no larger than a silver dollar. Across the face of it he placed a bit of stick about a foot in length, and, turning it to the proper angle with the needle, he would, in a rough way, sight forward to some prominent tree, as far in advance as could be discerned in the thick woods. Then the march would be made, in single file, to that tree; and then another sight forward would be taken, and the march resumed; and so on making successive stations.

Hour after hour the journey was continued without incident or variety. A slight pause at noon for lunch gave opportunity to discuss the mishaps that might occur. Was it certain that it would be easy to find the way back again through all this depth of woods? Jule explained, that, with the compass, the return would be very easy and sure. Even with so small an instrument there could be no important error. He did not know but there might be variations, but, if so, they balanced each other; for he had already found in his previous excursions, that, rough as the method with the stick and little needle was, it would always bring him back, when he reversed the course, to within a few rods of the original point of departure. There would be no difficulty in returning to the water-course.

The journey was resumed. It was the same monotonous march under the silent, sombre shadow of the vast forest. There was no change. Before two o'clock, the hard, steady plodding, began to tell upon the strength and vigor of the trio, and to dull the keen edge of expectation and excitement. At about that hour, however, an incident occurred which relieved the monotony. A mark along the ground was discovered. Following it a few rods, an old blaze with an axe upon a tree was seen. Immediately all was excitement and enthusiasm. It was apparent that here must be the trail of some hunter or trapper. Phil was confident that this was a path leading from a lake known to lie to the eastward, across to the twin-lakes. He urged, that, if its course could be traced, it should be followed. There was some opposition to this, because the trail, if it was one, did not seem to run in the direction the party were travelling. It was finally decided, however, Ed giving the casting vote, to follow it toward the right, if possible, for at least half an hour.

So the bushes were twisted and locked together across the little path, and some pieces of limbs piled up upon it, in order, that, upon returning, the point where the compass course struck the trail might be found again; for in the monotony of the vast wilderness, a point cannot be identified without marking it, any more than a place can be found upon the surface of the sea. After passing around a slight elevation, it was discovered that the trail ran in about the direction required, and it grew plainer as the party advanced. The walking was much easier. The excitement was renewed. The discoverers hastened forward with great expectation and delight, hoping every moment to see the woods grow lighter, and soon to see the lakes. There was a boyish rivalry as to who should first get a glimpse of the new world they were seeking. As they advanced, objects of interest began to appear. They came upon queer, grotesque heaps of rocks; and, just beyond, a jagged precipice suddenly burst upon them through an opening in the trees. Above the precipice, a forest-clad mountain rose, dark and magnificent. Against the blue sky, and against the mountain-side, an eagle was circling near the spruce-covered summit.

They stood for a while, and gazed with delight, and then, with fresh courage, resumed their journey. They thought the twin-lakes were certainly very near. The rough, rocky country and the mountain answered the description that had been given them before they began the journey. The trail led them along near the base of the precipice for a long distance, and then a little to the right, and away from it, and up upon a ridge, from which they could gain glimpses here and there of a narrow valley still farther to the right, and another ridge beyond. It was clear that the twin-lakes would be likely to be found between these two ridges. Expectation was therefore upon tiptoe. The fatigue of the nine hours' steady marching that had been accomplished was forgotten in the eagerness and keen excitement. It was a swift walk, and almost a run, as they hurried along the trail, each desirous of being the first to see the lakes.

An Adirondack Neighborhood

It was about five o'clock when Ed's quick eyes first discovered the blue gleam of water through the dark, thick branches, down in a valley to the right. With a joyful cry he proclaimed, "Hurrah the lakes!" His companions looked downward where he pointed; and then, with a shout, the little party broke from the trail, and rushed, sliding and tumbling, down to the blue water. It was less than a quarter of a mile down, and they did not stop to take breath until they had reached the very margin. It proved to be the waters for which they were searching. It was the larger of the twin-lakes. It was little (perhaps not half a mile in diameter); but it was a gem of beauty. Embedded in the mountains, and circled with the rich green of the virgin forest, it seemed to the young adventures a place of enchantment. They looked, and listened, and wondered.

The stillness of the forest was here very remarkable. As the party stood upon the narrow line of clear, yellow sand which formed the beach of the lake, the chipper and movements of a red squirrel away across the water sounded preposterously loud, and almost alarming; and, when a sharp blow was struck upon a rock with a stick, it shivered the silence with a shock and an echo that seemed intrusive and painful.

Near the place where the youthful adventurers reached the lake, they found a low bark structure, about four feet by six, open at one side, and evidently used at some period as a hunter's shanty. It was merely a small, low, open bark shed, under which three persons could recline, with their feet to a camp-fire outside. It seemed old, as if abandoned long ago. No marks of human footsteps had been seen upon the trail, and none were visible about the shanty. Upon looking inside, a small, rough outline of a man in a boat was discovered, drawn with a pencil upon the smooth bark: under it were the names of two men, and the statement that they were hunters, and built the shanty. The date, some four years back, was also given. Near the shanty, at the water's edge, were some dried pieces of dead cedar-trees, thrown together in a way that led to the inference that they had once formed a raft.

A camp-fire was soon made in front of the shanty, and the raft was re-arranged. Two fishing-poles were cut with a jack-knife from the bushes, the lines and bait which had been brought along were produced, and then Ed and Phil floated out upon the lake. The raft would barely sustain the two. They reached the line of lily-pads which circled round the lake. There was an inlet near: opposite this they commenced fishing. The trout were ready and eager. There was a pleasant excitement in taking them; but no special skill was required. A stout cord, with a hook on the end and a worm on it, was the tackle employed. This was the method customarily used in that section, and the only one known to the young fishermen. It was very efficient. In a few minutes they returned to the shore with an abundant supply of trout.

Wood for the fire during the night, and spruce-boughs for a bed under the shanty, were hastily gathered; and the little party, very tired and hungry, sat down to supper. A few pounds of cornmeal, a little salt, a basin, a square piece of tin, and an iron spoon, constituted the whole outfit they had brought with them. In the basin a batter was made; and meal-cakes were cooked on the tin placed over the coals. But the principal food was trout. Spitted upon sticks, and broiled, the fish were delicious.

After supper, the party reclined upon the spruce-boughs under the shanty, with their feet to the fire and watched the dark night-shadows settle down around them. The deep recesses of the damp evergreen forest grew utterly black, only a few tree-trunks near by being visible by the light of the fire. Uneasy glances were turned now and then toward the darkness. Jule fell back upon his knowledge of natural history, as usual, and stated that there was no well-authenticated instance of any wild animal in the Adirondack forest, except, possibly, wolves in winter, ever making a voluntary attack upon a human being. There was further talk of this kind; then drowsiness began, and the conversation ceased. Suddenly there was a "swish," and a swoop across the little circle of firelight, which startled the drowsy party, and made the pulses beat, and every nerve tingle in this wild place. It was only an owl of a peculiar variety, which Jule named, but which is now forgotten. It had a white breast, that shone in the ruddy firelight like silver. The silent bird alighted upon a limb, and gazed for a while in stupid wonder at the glowing embers, then fluttered away into the gloom of the forest.

After this incident, the party again stretched themselves out upon the spruce-boughs under the shanty, with their feet to the fire; and, in spite of loneliness and imaginary terrors, vigorous youth and excessive fatigue accomplished their work, and the boys slept. Some time in the night Phil awoke. The fire was low, and it was very dark. A sense of the dreariness and desolation of the vast forest solitude swept over him with a strange and thrilling power. A few giant pines that reached away up above the rest of the woods were sighing. The midnight voices that he heard, and seemed to hear, were the deepest and saddest that had ever spoken to the boy's spirit, and he remembered them afterwards as unequalled in all his subsequent experience.

Phil replenished the fire, and again went to rest beside his two companions, who were breathing heavily in deep slumber.

The morning broke bright and cheerful. It was one of those rare golden days that come only in September. But the boys did not stir abroad very much. The fact was, they were thoroughly jaded and worn out by the excessive work of the previous day. They did only that which was necessary. They caught fish, and cooked them for breakfast, noticing, in the mean time, how very cold it was in this solitude. The leaves along the lake-shore were stiff and brittle with the film of ice formed upon

An Adirondack Neighborhood 73

them by the freezing of the mist that rose from the water.

After breakfast the boys slept until noon, and then fished and cooked and ate, and then slept again. But young blood was triumphant, and they were soon recuperated. By three o'clock in the afternoon they were standing upon the shore of the lake, cracking jokes, and looking at the deer-tracks in the sand, and wondering. They saw a huge black bird come flapping lazily along high up in the air, and knew by its dismal croak that it must be a raven. They also saw a fowl floating away up in a lane of water, at the farthest point in view, and heard a shrill cry which they at once knew must be that of a loon. It sounded so loud with its echo, that it seemed as if the entire timber upon the side of the mountain was tumbling down.

A little before sundown, Ed and Phil floated out again to fish. They had just reached the lily-pads, and arranged their lines, when they heard a soft "Hist!" come over the still water from the camp. They looked back, and on the beach stood Jule, with his arm pointing out toward a narrow belt of wild grass that bordered the farther shore of the lake; and they heard him pronounce in a clear whisper the word "*Deer!*"

The fishermen looked, and recognized a light tawny color on the grass-belt; and a moment after it moved, and the deer raised her head, and looked around. Then she put her head down, and commenced feeding again. It was a thrilling moment. To reach the shore and get the rifle was the first suggestion. A moment later, a glance revealed that Jule had procured the weapon, and stood ready with it in his hand.

The fishermen commenced moving their craft toward the shore. In the excitement a slight noise was made. The deer raised her head. "Do not move a finger," whispered Phil fiercely. Ed had his pole half raised; but he remained rigidly in that position. The deer, after looking a moment, put her head down in the grass again.

The two raftsmen reached the beach, and secured the rifle. It was Ed's property; but, with a generosity I cannot pause to praise sufficiently he insisted upon giving it up, upon this important occasion, to the elder and more practised marksman.

Phil accepted the responsibility, and planned the campaign. He directed Ed to navigate the raft as noiselessly as possible across the lake, in the direction of the game. Phil gathered himself down into a little heap, so as to rest the rifle to the best advantage; and then the voyage commenced. Whenever the deer raised her head from the long grass, the voyagers were statues. When her head was down, Ed was silently doing his utmost to propel the floating platform across the lake.

When they had reached the centre of the lake, the water was very deep, so that the setting-pole could only be used as a sort of oar or paddle. But the cedar composing the raft was very light, and good progress was made.

Notwithstanding the excitement, Phil, being inactive in his recumbent position, found himself, not only watching the deer, but wondering at the beauty of the lake, which burst upon him unexpectedly, as seen from its central point. Around him was the circular expanse of water-lilies, and beyond that was a narrow belt of yellowish-green wild-grass, then a circle of low tamarack-trees of a deeper tinge, and then the black-green of the spruce-forest, stretching away up the mountain-sides. Back beyond the camp was a high peak, which had been hidden from those near the shore, but which now suddenly came out into view, its dark mass looming up with startling boldness and nearness against the clear blue sky. Phil was thrilled through and through with this sudden revelation of grandeur and beauty.

Fifteen minutes' voyaging brought the two navigators within a couple of hundred yards of the deer. This would have been an exceedingly long shot,—too distant to make sure work with any rifle; but at this point Ed became anxious. "Shoot, Phil, shoot!" was whispered many times from the rear of the raft. But Phil remained quiet and immovable, with rifle pointing toward the deer. The raft continued to advance. The deer raised her head, and seemed uneasy.

"Shoot, shoot! she is going," whispered Ed excitedly, but very softly.

The deer's eyes could now be distinguished. This was the sign that had been waited for. It had been said by hunters that this indicated rifle-range. It was also said that ordinarily a new hand would miss about twenty deer before killing one. Phil was very anxious to do his best the first time. The deer favored him. She put her head down to feed again. The raft floated to within about one hundred and twenty yards. The deer, in her feeding, turned and presented a broadside. Then the signal was given to cease propelling the raft, and remain perfectly still. Phil knew that he had a difficult task to perform. In the first place, the sights of the little rifle were calculated for a very short range. He knew, that, for the longer range he was taking, he must allow at least eight inches for the falling of the bullet in going the distance. He knew that he must hit near the heart to kill. He felt that the chances, resting as he was on a crazy little raft in the water, were not in his favor. Perhaps his knowledge of these difficulties, and the probability of failing, rendered him cool and collected. He was a fine marksman when shooting at a target, and that was his hope now. He settled himself in position, and drew a bead just under the backbone of the deer, at the point where the lighter color indicated the shoulder.

He paused for a favorable moment. The water was glassy, and the raft was perfectly still. Phil closed his eyes for an instant to have them fresh, then opened them, sighted keenly and steadily, and pulled.

The sharp crack of the rifle rang out, and was echoed back in long crashes from the mountainsides. The deer was seen to give two jumps, and was then hidden behind the long grass.

"That deer is hit," said Ed, now in a full excited tone, relieved from the necessity of whispering.

Then Ed went on to say that he had watched the white brush of the deer's tail intently; for, according to the hunter's creed, if that white flag is lowered, it is a hit. He had noticed, that, when the rifle cracked, the white flag went down with a jerk.

The raft was brought up to the edge of the wildgrass. Phil went to step off upon it; but here was a difficulty. At its outer margin this grassy belt was of that singular kind which seems to float upon water. It would undulate in waves, like the surface of the lake, and would not support a footstep. Pieces of cedar from the raft had to be laid over it; and, walking upon these, Phil gained the firmer grassy formation. He advanced toward the lines of bushes. Just where the long grass joined the tamaracks, he saw a light tawny color in the green; and another step revealed to his delighted vision the deer, lying perfectly still in her wild, enchanting beauty. He shouted the success back to his comrades; and the manifestations of joy that ensued were very extravagant.

The deer was slid over the grass to the waters' edge, and floated behind the raft to camp. Jule supervised the dressing of the game. He announced that the little bullet had passed through the aorta close to the heart.

I will not pursue the account of our adventures further. I will only add, in regard to the Adirondack neighborhood, that it is pleasant to know one place that is substantially permanent in its appearance. The farms and woodlands remain the same. It is pleasant, also, to find there from year to year, as I visit it, but few changes among the people.

An Adirondack Home

Far off, crossing the vast, dim valley below us, the St. Lawrence River is seen,—a thread of silver creeping through the verdure to the sea.

We are at an Adirondack homestead, where I spend a part of every summer. It is a remote place among the mountains, and just in the edge of the great woods. My brother Edward now resides here.

In the bottom of a deep, wooded valley, through which flows our little river, a quarter of a mile back of the house, is the saw-mill. We (three brothers) built it when we were boys. We still treasure a large flat bottle filled with sawdust,—the first cut by the saw, when the mill was started, more than twenty years ago. In order to comprehend the sentiment involved in this sawdust, it is important to know that we picked out this place in the forest, and paid for it by our industry, and built the mill, from ground-sills to ridgepole, including the machinery and everything about it, with our own youthful hands. We were millwrights, carpenters, and builders, learning the trades as we went along.

The rest of the farm is now cleared, but we still keep

the deep valley in woods, as it was in the good old times. It is a very cool, leafy retreat in summer, and many old associations are connected with it.

In coming here for my vacation, I brought with me from the city my office-boy, Salsify Kamfer, aged fourteen, a slim and handsome lad, with a sweet face, brown eyes, and dark hair.

I learned early in our journey that the care of this city boy in the country was likely to be enlivening. Although a docile Sabbath-school scholar at home, and full of good impulses, his city-bred soul revolted against the country. As we left metropolitan surroundings and the railroad dwindled to a single track and the telegraph to a single wire and the stations to mere sheds of rough boards, Salsify could not forbear expressions of contempt. He also told me very frankly that the people were the most disagreeable he had ever seen. He said they were afraid to talk. When I explained to him that quiet living in solitary places induced habits of taciturnity and reserve, he insisted that it was not reserve, but sulkiness.

The morning after our arrival, when I endeavored to impress Salsify with a sense of the grandeur of the landscape that stretches away to a dim horizon in Canada, he conceded all I claimed for it, but was evidently much more interested in a couple of guinea-fowls that were rambling about the door-yard with the chickens and turkeys. We were informed that these "guineas" kept the hawks off. The harsh clangor of their voices was supposed to have this effect. But Salsify was chiefly interested in the fact that the guineas were great fighters. He remarked that their heads were more like snakes' heads than like the heads of other fowls. When, two days after our arrival, it was discovered that the male guinea had a leg broken and the big Plymouth Rock rooster had lost an eye in a mutual unpleasantness, Salsify began to manifest for the first time a genuine respect for the country. The female guinea has an ugly trick which interests the boy. When quietly feeding near the chickens, she suddenly brings her reptilian head to a level, pointing toward a chicken, and then, making a rush, strikes the unsuspecting victim. The feathers fly, also the chicken. After suffering a few attacks of this kind, the persecuted innocent begins to limp, and eventually grows weak in the back and dies.

Salsify, in a dim, unconscious way, sympathizes with the guinea-fowls. He admires their neat appearance and their exhibitions of power. They resemble the city demagogue, who stands for the boy's idea of a hero.

If Salsify is in fault in his admiration, perhaps I am equally so in mine. My favorite is the tall, gaunt, bluish-gray fox-hound who guards the house and premises. This dog, Plato by name, has an enemy the strangest and most absurd that ever afflicted a quadruped. He has battled with it for many years. The bitterness of these contests has sunk deep into his mentality, and is now apparent in his long, melancholy visage. His enemy is not a burglar or another dog: it is simply and vaguely the thunder of the heavens. Plato's battles with the thunder-storms are widely known and often talked of in the neighborhood. As we came here in the heart of the summer, I have had opportunity to see Plato in full operation.

As the first low muttering of a storm is heard, Plato's warm brown eyes, which I have perhaps just then caressed into a peaceful and affectionate expression, darken and contract, the wrinkles on his face deepen, his long, slim tail suddenly becomes a crow-bar, and, jerking away from me and throwing his head, his mouth opens, and the long, moaning, bell-like note peculiar to his race echoes through the clearing. If he happens to be in the house, it makes no difference: his voice cannot be suppressed. The only relief is to get him out as soon as possible. He is, presumably, inspired with the vision of grisly terror from the moment he hears the thunder coming. This thing has apparently become the nightmare of his existence.

Having uttered his premonitory howl, Plato's next proceeding is to dash off as far as the boundary line of the premises. Here he stations himself, and pours out his soul in long, dismal, defiant notes, facing the storm. As each fresh peal is heard, his excitement increases, until he runs at his utmost speed, tearing from side to side along the line, throwing his head skyward, and pouring out great volleys of sound against the advancing foe. During these exercises, Plato (who is in all else a very obedient dog) is equally regardless of entreaties and threats, or even blows. He seems to remember only that the family and the premises must be protected, and that he alone is responsible.

As the storm progresses and crosses the line of battle, a scene ensues generally designated and known as "Plato's circus." It is evidently clear to him that his enemies are coming in all directions. He turns this way and that to repel and pursue them. The dog's ambition is apparently to catch always the last thunder-bolt before it has time to leave the clearing. In this mad pursuit he charges around the house and across the premises in all directions in a howling frenzy of excitement. As the deluge comes down, Plato may be dimly seen through the sheets of water flitting past, drawing himself out into a blue line in his efforts to increase his speed sufficiently to overtake that last thunder-bolt. As the bolts come thicker and faster, Plato's howl is sometimes broken short off, ending with a squeak, as he twists himself to a sharp angle, leaving the old and turning to pursue the new arrival. In the midst of such terrors his voice also becomes "choky," and seems almost articulate in its expression, this effect being due doubtless to his feelings and to the fact that his mouth is likely to be partly filled with rain-water.

Frequently it becomes evident that Plato is, in his own opinion, getting the worst of it. The contest upon his part degenerates into almost a squabble. The strange, invisible powers of the air press heavily upon his imagination. There is a tradition that when very young he was sometimes driven to the barn with drooping tail and scared wits by an unusually sharp clap of thunder. But in later years, although at times almost pulverized by fear, he has never retreated. He not only maintains his ground, but makes a point of always pursuing the last bellowing monster until its voice dies away behind the hills.

When all is over, the poor dog comes into the house whimpering and whining like a sick child, begging for sympathy, and evidently under the impression that he has warded off a dreadful calamity. It is now past the middle of the dog-days. Plato has become worn and haggard. Thunder-storms are frequent. He no sooner subdues one than another more hideous and awful is discovered stealing insidiously upon him from behind the horizon. Like all his race, however, he is very enduring; and it is the general impression that he will be able to continue, as in previous years, with forces unabated, to the close of the summer campaign.

One of Plato's peculiarities is that his intelligence resides chiefly in his nose. He refuses to accept the testimony of his eyes unsupported by his more trustworthy nasal organ. He has even failed to recognize his master at sight; and usually on meeting any of the family away from home he circles around to the leeward and takes a sniff before making his approaches.

Plato is at his best when hunting the foxes which abound in the neighborhood. He never hunts them alone, but always in company with his cousin Hero, who belongs upon an adjoining farm. The exploits of the two dogs are noteworthy. The pair, when allowed to go at large, are well-mated vagabonds. If not prevented, they would do nothing but hunt foxes all the year round,—except, of course, at such times as Plato is engaged in his thunder-storm business. To prevent an extensive waste of dog-power, Hero is, as a rule, kept chained at home. Plato, however, is at liberty to visit him at any time and cheer him with reminiscenses or with the hope of a good time coming. The good time always comes in the autumn. When the summer heats are over and the golden brown of October appears, it is proper and decorous to chase the foxes. On a fine frosty morning Hero is unchained and permitted his freedom. It is a joyful moment indeed to the two friends. There is an immense wagging of tails, and a manifestation of hilarity that seems a little out of place in dogs of so grave and solemn a character as these hounds are.

Within fifteen minutes after Hero is liberated, the two friends start upon their first hunt of the season. They generally go first to a piece of woods at the east of the house and about a mile distant. Usually within half an hour the first wild yelp announcing a fresh track is heard. A few minutes later, the fox, closely followed by Plato, is seen crossing a long level which is just beyond the road in front of the house. The foxes, having had rest from dogs since the previous autumn or winter, are not very shy. Last autumn the first fox started in this manner seemed almost to have been caught napping, for

Plato was close upon his heels. As they were seen crossing the wide, open stretch of meadow, it seemed inevitable that Plato, who is a very fast dog, would catch the game; but the fox was a very cunning animal and a great dodger. As we looked upon the race from the piazza, it was jump and dodge and squirm and twist and zigzag all across the field, until at last Reynard reached a rail-fence at the boundary. Here the fox had a trick which gave him an advantage. He went through the fence, and the dog went through after him. Then the fox dodged back again to the other side of the fence, and so continued threading the fence back and forth like a needle, and the dog, trying to follow with his greater bulk, was embarrassed and confused. The fox, skittering along the line of fence in this alternate manner, secured a respectable start, and the dog was left behind to pick up the track and follow the scent in the usual way, which he did with eager yelps and howlings. In the mean time, the heavy "boom, boom" of old Hero's voice, as he steadily and soberly followed the track across the meadow and along the fence, would have told any expert in these matters that Hero, though the slower dog, had better staying qualities. Hero had been in at the death of a great many deer, a few bears, one catamount, and a variety of other game, in his years of hunting among the Adirondack Mountains. It is observable that he now leaves all the lighter play and circling-round to his less experienced friend, while he himself follows along the regular line.

An Adirondack Home

In some instances the men of the family at our farmhouse, induced by the entreating voices of the dogs, go out with their guns to secure the fox. The method is to listen to the course the dogs are taking, and to stand in the line of approach. Ere long the fugitive will be seen coming, and he will approach until within easy range, if the hunter remains quiet. In this way many foxes are secured each year. But in the majority of instances the two dogs are not seconded by the men. Then they go chasing on and baying hour after hour, until they have worn out the day, and perhaps the night, in the pursuit.

Sometimes the fox, tired of the chase, takes to his hole. The men, hearing the baying at a fixed point, know what has happened. Occasionally they go to the assistance of the dogs. Then, with a long withe or pole, cut from the woods, they explore to find the direction of the hole, and, cutting down from above, reach the fox in his home. In unearthing the fox there is usually a tussle. Plato, in an agony of excitement, perceiving by his exquisite sense of smell that the fox is just in advance of the shovels, in spite of all prohibitions dives in among the implements, crams his long, slim head into the hole, and a moment later, with a smothered yell, pulls backward. What has happened? The little hunted fugitive has turned upon his pursuer and has planted his small, sharp, foxy teeth in the most sensitive part of that wonderful nose which is Plato's grandest characteristic. Plato continues to pull and yell, and the fox, finally, rather than be drawn out into open day, lets go. Plato's nose has become quite crooked in consequence of these encounters. The shovels resume. Then old Hero comes up warily, and, as the fox is unearthed, Hero's ponderous jaws close upon poor Reynard's cranium, and it is crushed like an egg-shell; and the men, saying that there is "one varmint the less" in the neighborhood to kill the turkeys, go triumphantly home.

There is another issue which often results to the hounds from "holing" a fox. The men occasionally pay no attention to their beseechings, but leave the two canine friends to their own devices. In that case Plato sometimes turns himself into an excavator. He uses his strong fore-legs and broad paws in digging. Holes made by his work and running several yards into the hill-side have been discovered. Notwithstanding his uniform failures to reach the game by this method, he continues to practice the art of digging with unabated enthusiasm. The notion that he will ultimately dig out a fox is evidently one of his cherished hallucinations.

The tenacity and endurance of the hounds are best seen when they are left wholly to themselves in their hunting, as they often are for weeks together. They will be absent from home upon one of their "hunting sprees" for perhaps thirty-six hours, and engaged during all that time in the chase, pursuing by night as well as by day. Plato returning from such a dissipation is a sight to see. He went away full-fleshed and sleek; he returns a mere sack of bones, so terrific have been the excitement and exertion. If it is cold and wet, as it is apt to be in this mountain region in autumn, he is permitted to come into the kitchen and lie down behind the stove with the cat. For a season he is merely sluggish clay, sleeping constantly, or waking only to eat voraciously or to avoid the broom of the housewife. After about three days he is recuperated, and starts off again, fresh as ever, to meet his cousin Hero, doubtless by appointment, and the pair set out for another episode in their wild career. Such a life would speedily destroy any animal organization less enduring than that of the hound.

The gentle side of Plato's nature is best seen in his dealings with Miss Sylvia, the cat. As we are sitting upon the piazza, a gleam of pure milk-white comes whirling and dancing suddenly around the corner of the house upon the green lawn. A glance tells us that it is Miss Sylvia in pursuit of some imaginary object. As she sees her canine friend recumbent at our feet, with a quick, joyful step and serious air she comes up on the piazza to greet him. She is a very affectionate creature. She advances to Plato slowly, and, softly purring, walks directly under his raised head, touches his jowls with her arched back, and coquetishly flirts her tail in his face. Then she turns and walks backward and forward, purring and rubbing her furry sides against his throat and breast, while he elevates his nose a little disdainfully to give her room to pass. If he still remains stern and cold—as he usually does—and utterly regardless, she then looks up in his face, raises her right forepaw daintily and gives a soft pat with it upon one of his long, pendulous, silken ears. This, as Salsify says, generally "fetches him." Plato rises and glances upward at us sheepishly, as if he would say, "What does she want with me? I despise this nonsense;" and then he puts his long nose down against Miss Puss and gently pushes her off the piazza on to the grass. Then Plato returns and sits gravely down by us upon his haunches with a very dignified air, as if he had performed an important family duty. Miss Puss endures this cheerfully. She is evidently a little afraid to trifle with her friend, and quite willing to be treated by him as an inferior if she can retain his good opinion. It is quite clear, also, that Plato is a little ashamed of the sentimentality of their friendship. It is asserted that upon one occasion when Miss Sylvia was unusually familiar Plato went so far as to take her in his mouth and drop her into a tub of rain-water which stands just at the corner of the house; but, upon cross-examination, the evidence of this did not seem to be sufficient. There can be no doubt, however, that Plato does not like publicly to own his friendship for the cat. He would unquestionably be very unwilling to have his cousin Hero know of it.

I have not been able to impress Salsify with my ideas of Plato. He regards "that fool of a dog" as a failure. Salsify is to me a perpetual delight. His utter ignorance of the different varieties of trees and of the birds we see is amazing.

As soon as we came here I established a little camp for picnicking about a mile below the mill, in the deep, wooded ravine through which flows the river. Here Salsify and I have spent many of the warmest days, entirely free from the heat. We occupy the time with fishing, conversation, reading, and athletic games. We have but few callers: a solitary crane hangs round, and a kingfisher claims an adverse possession. We could easily take along the rifle which is at the house and kill the kingfisher and the crane, and perhaps some of the red and black squirrels that frequent the cool, wooded valley; but we are both opposed to such proceedings, and object to them when they are suggested by our country friends. As we sit on the piazza at the house with the family and the neighbors in the cool of the day, and talk of our little camp where we picnic, and of farming, and hunting, and other topics, there is greater freedom and enjoyment than I have known anywhere else, except, perhaps, among the girls and boys at a district school. The families of the neighborhood seem to constitute only one large family. They run in and out and about each other's houses as if they were common property. Salsify is beginning to enjoy this free life, and says he never found so much pleasure in any other. The freedom of the place has extended to our camp, rendering the long talks which Salsify and I enjoy there free and confidential. My own burden—the knowledge that life is so far advanced with me and I have accomplished so little—has been placed frankly before my office-boy during the days we have spent together in the leafy solitude of the woods lying on the bank of the river. We have also read a few books together; but there is a difference in our tastes which works against success in this direction: he still clings to sea-stories and delights in piratical adventures. We get along better in relating our experiences. He exerts himself to impress me with a sense of the daring character of his adventures. The days at school when he "licked" all the other boys, and the days in the streets when he fought with the "mudlarks" and was himself "covered with gore" and glory, are dwelt upon for my edification.

This extravagant talk on the part of Salsify has to be taken with a good deal of allowance. He is a fine young chap, with generous impulses, and his reckless boasting is in part the result of a pardonable purpose. For this youth is trying to ward off what he regards as a dire calamity, and he thinks this kind of talk may help him.

The calamity which Salsify dreads, and the fear of which is a burden to him, is the imputation of goodness. Vague as the danger is, and perhaps to most minds shadowy, it is as much a reality to him as my burden is to me, or the thunder-storm to Plato. It appears that on several occasions at the Sunday-school and elsewhere Salsify has been called "a good boy." No other appellation could so humiliate or depress him. "I am no saint," he pleads indignantly, as he discourses of his grievance in our camp. And then he proceeds to lay before me the lies he has told, the battles he has fought, and the small thefts he has committed. I discover also that he has a list of semi-profane words, which he explodes like firecrackers in his vehement talk. In reply to Salsify I am compelled to admit that, taking all the sins together which he has committed since his babyhood, the array is perhaps sufficient to constitute a barrier against goodness. But I do not tell him that which I cannot help thinking,—that, with his extremely impulsive nature, sweet disposition, and honesty of purpose, he is not likely wholly to escape the imputation which he so much dreads.

Salsify's criticism of those who have been his instructors at school is interesting. "There is Miss Williams," he exclaims patronizingly, "who might be a real nice girl, but she is a slave to duty, and has no more idea of freedom or a good time than a machine."

I suggest that she is discreet.

He replies that she makes an old hen of herself, and that if any one has got to be always discreet like that, it is no use to live.

I remark that I have heard her speak well of him.

"Yes," says Salsify, a little conceitedly, "I know she likes me." And then, after a moment's reflection, he adds indignantly, "I don't like her: she thinks I am good: she thinks I am a little tin angel on wheels."

Two miles east of our farm-house, on a hillside, is a small hut, which can be distinctly seen in a clear day, and which is brought out very plainly by using a spy-glass. This hut interests Salsify and the rest of us, because it is the hunting-lodge of the Alaska-saple-man. (The word sable is always pronounced *saple* in this region.)

The authorities in such matters here say that of

course there is no such animal as the Alaska saple; but they add, with a laugh, that the fur of the Alaska saple is obtained from an odorous animal not convenient to stumble over on moonlight nights. The fur of the Alaska saple in the market might not seem as sweet by another name. Therefore there is, as a convenient fiction, such an animal as the Alaska saple, and his fur is very fine, and happens now to be in fashion.

For some months in autumn and winter the Alaska-saple-man pursues his lucrative calling. He lives a hermit-life, and is not likely to be troubled with visitors. At the termination of his exile he deodorizes himself, his dog, and his peltry, manages to get into a new suit of clothes at some intermediate point, and returns to his fellow-beings.

I have not stated hitherto the fact that our little camp and general location are in and near a belt of woods which connects (with some slight breaks caused by clearings) the Adirondack forest with the forests of Canada. More or less deer are seen every season passing over this territory or run-way in their journeyings, and now and then a bear is discovered along the same line. These are often pursued and killed. Sometimes the hunt and capture are in sight of the houses. The story of each of these incidents is valued as an important part of the history of the neighborhood. The oldest bear-story relates a capture four miles away, at the Corners. There is a small church at the Corners. Soon after it was built, forty years ago, one Sunday, while the people were in church, they heard suddenly a great noise outside on the green. Looking out, they saw an immense black bear, fighting with three dogs. The meeting closed unceremoniously, and the people went out to see the fight. In a few minutes the hunters who were pursuing came up, and the bear was killed.

It would require a pretty thick volume to set forth the store of good things in the way of hunting adventures and incidents which have accumulated in our neighborhood within the last thirty years. They can be told worthily only by the hunters themselves, in the cool Adirondack summer twilight or by the winter fireside.

Salsify's interest in the narrations we heard of hunting-exploits evening after evening on the piazza, the first week after our arrival, was extreme. Moved by curiosity and the stories, he naturally desired to explore, and resolved, among other things, to attend church at the Corners, where that bear was killed on the green. On Sunday morning, before I was aware of it, he had arrayed himself and had gone alone to the place. He returned early in the afternoon, and explained to me that the church-services did not amount to anything, and that he had never been so stared at in all his life before. He professed, however, not to care for the staring, and said he could look any man, woman, or child of them all, including the preacher, out of countenance in ten seconds.

I did not venture at the time to tell Salsify why he

had attracted so much attention. I enlightened him gradually in the course of the week, as I thought he could bear it. When I had told him all, he was, to my surprise, not abashed, but pleased, and gloried in the sensation he had created. The fact was, he had decked himself out in what he supposed to be real country style. Whether he had gained his ideas from Buffalo Bill as seen on the stage, or from some book, I did not learn. However it was, he had brought the things with him in his trunk and his suit consisted of blue flannel pants, a handsome blue flannel shirt, with broad collar and silver stars, and a pair of brilliant red suspenders, without coat or vest. It was a neat rig for fancy yachting, or for a hero on the stage; but for a quiet little country church, in which there were not five people who had ever seen the sea or a theatre, it was not quite the thing certainly. I learned afterward that Salsify was variously taken by the plain people who saw him for a drummer-boy, a sailor, an actor, an escaped circus-performer, and a vender of patent medicines.

As Salsify came to know of these misapprehensions, he rejoiced in them, and was delighted with the sensation he had produced.

The next Sabbath, when I went with him to the same church, he urged so strongly his right to wear the brilliant suit again that (with some modifications) it was permitted. I noticed that he sat during the entire service in a belligerent attitude, breathing defiance. The religious exercises, simple and majestic in their homely setting, entirely failed to reach down to the current of his youthful life. His imaginary contest with the worshipers entirely absorbed him.

Another of Salsify's explorations consisted in seeing how near he could get to the hut of the Alaska-sapleman. With this object in view, he wandered off alone, intending to make his way through the woods in a direct line to the locality. He was absent all day, and returned from "somewhere down toward Canada," having gone astray. Coming out on a road, he paid a man who knew the country a dollar and a half to bring him home, where he arrived after nightfall.

Perhaps it was this experience on the part of Salsify that led him and all of us to take so deep an interest in the boy who was lost near Blue Mountain. Blue Mountain is about twenty miles from where we are located. The news that a boy was lost in the woods spread very rapidly. The huckleberry-plains at the foot of the mountain are visited every year by farmers who come with their families, and camp in this wild section and pick berries, and make a holiday time of it. The boy who was lost, Andrew Garfield by name, was in one of these camps. He went out toward evening to hunt partridges, and did not come back. His parents and the camps were, of course, alarmed. Quite a disturbance was made, and a good many people were said to have gone to the place next day. The second day after Andrew disappeared, my brother Edward and Salsify and I went to the scene. Edward drove his team, taking us with him in a rough lumber-wagon. The twenty miles of road we traveled was smooth and hard, and the bright air and mountain-landscapes were a perpetual enjoyment.

Edward gave a man who was walking in our direction a ride. This custom of giving a ride to any one on foot is universal in the locality. The man who accepted the ride was named Sam Curley. Mr. Curley said there was a new joke down where he lived. Tom Powell had sold a cow to Bill Worden for a six-year-old animal, when she was no such thing. The cow had only one horn. Bill looked at his purchase and noticed that there were thirteen wrinkles on her horn. One wrinkle comes every year: so that it appeared to him the cow must be thirteen years old. He felt bad about it, and spoke to Tom, charging that Tom had misrepresented the age of the animal. Tom replied indignantly, asking Bill if he really was such a numskull and did not know anything. "Why," said Tom, "the animal has but one horn, and of course both wrinkles come on one horn." Bill had to accept the explanation.

About an hour before noon we reached the huckleberry-plains. We found a dozen little tents clustered together, and there were twenty or thirty teams and nearly a hundred people. It was on the bank of the St. Regis River. There was a fine view of the mountain, and miles and miles of woods stretching away in every direction.

The story about the lost boy was that, he having gone after the partridges and not returning, a dozen men had gone into the woods that same night, making more or less noise, and trying to call loud enough for the boy to hear them. But they could do nothing. The tall, raw-boned man, with red hair, who answered our questions, said they might as well have tried to walk right through a mountain of tar as to go through "them woods" that night.

On the following morning four parties of men, with guns, had gone into the woods in four different directions and commenced firing the guns. There was one solitary report of a gun heard, apparently in reply, far off up the river, but after that no response. As they could not find the boy, two surveyors had been sent for, and in the afternoon of the day after the boy was lost the surveyors arrived. They were familiar with the entire region. They said the boy was probably wandering off up the river, and the single report of a gun which had been heard in reply was from *his* gun. They took a party of four men, with provisions, and immediately plunged into the woods.

When we arrived upon the scene, the boy had been out one day and two nights (about forty hours), and the surveyors had been nearly twenty-four hours in the woods. We pitched the little tent we had brought, tied our horses to the back end of the wagon, where they could feed from the wagon-box, and made ourselves at home among the huckleberry-pickers and those who were waiting to hear from the lost boy.

In the evening it was pleasant at the camps. Fires were built in front of some of the tents, and the men, gathering round them, chatted, and a few sung songs. Some of the older ones talked of old times on the Potomac. They said camping revived memories of their days in the army.

About an hour after dark there was an exciting incident. The report of a rifle was heard a quarter of a mile away in the bush. It was replied to by several of the men at the camps by discharging guns and by loud calls. A few minutes later two men came out of the woods, saying they had felt their way in the intense blackness for two hours, having almost reached the camps before dark. They were two of the men who had gone out with surveyors. As the people gathered round them and listened with breathless interest, they explained that the surveyors had come upon the track of the boy and were following it up the river in a line parallel with the stream and about two miles distant from it. They had followed the track about six miles when the two men were sent back with the news. The men said they saw where the boy had picked blueberries, and that there was no doubt that it was the track of Andrew.

At this point in the narrative a little shriek was heard, and attention was drawn to the shrieker. She was a compact little woman, with light hair and a neat blue calico dress. She was Andrew's mother. She was soothed by the other women. Her husband said, "Don't cry, Jane: maybe he ain't dead, after all."

After Jane and her husband had gone away to their tent, there was some discussion in regard to the probability of the boy being found alive. The red-haired man thought it would be possible. This man seemed to be an excitable individual. He declared that he would not sleep a wink that night, because he would be thinking all the while about Andrew.

The two men who had brought the intelligence said the surveyors had sent out word that the boy would very likely get to the bank of the river in his wandering, and they thought if he did he would keep along by the side of it. They wished, therefore, that some of the men would take a boat and go up the St. Regis River a dozen miles or more, searching and calling as they went. They thought it possible that the boy might be found in that way.

By midnight all had been said that could well be suggested, and the company around the fires dropped away to the tents to sleep. The next day was Sunday. It still remained clear and bright weather. The day was spent in various ways by the people, but the majority remained quietly at the camps. Divine service was suggested, but, on inquiry, it appeared that there was no one present who was willing to address the people or to lead them in religious exercises. There were, however, several good singers present, and groups of people spent a part of the day in singing Moody and Sankey hymns and other selections that they had in memory. Salsify somewhat distinguished himself in these exercises.

The great event of the day occurred at about five o'clock in the afternoon. It seemed that the red-haired man and a friend of his, acting on the suggestion of the surveyors, had taken a boat on Sunday morning at the dawn of day and had gone up the St. Regis River. As it was mostly "still water," they had penetrated a dozen miles or more along the river into the woods. Some time after noon they turned and came down the river again. A little while before five o'clock they had nearly got back to camp, and were coming around the last bend of the river, three quarters of a mile above the camps. There was some wild grass growing on the shore just at the bend. Something rustled, and then a boy put his head up above the grass: it was Andrew, the lost boy. He called out lustily, asking the men for a ride in the boat down to camp. Fifteen minutes later, down at camp, a hum, a buzz, a roar began off toward the river, and the next we knew there was the red-haired man and a handsome, light-haired boy with his cap off right in our midst and it was known that the boy was Andrew, who had been found. There we all were, shouting and crying and laughing. The first individual movement that I distinctly recall was that of the mother of Andrew. Coming from a tent, she rushed forward like a projectile from a catapult, but seemed to weaken after a moment, and actually fell down on her face in the midst of the tumult. She was helped up, and had a chance to put her arms about her boy's neck, after which she sat down on the ground and cried.

Immediately after this, attention was called to the red-haired man, who was making his arms go and trying to tell the story, how they had found the lad. "I tell you what, boys," said he, "when the grass wiggled and he put his head up and I see it was Andrew a-sittin' there, like little Moses in the bulrushes, it just made my hair pull."

Andrew, who was about Salsify's age, evidently did not like all this excitement. His mother's sympathy compelled him to cry a little, but it was clearly disagreeable to him. When asked if he was starved, he said no, he was not hungry much.

Andrew's supper was not long in coming. He was annoyed by the attention bestowed upon him while eating. After supper he admitted that he had been "a little bit holler" toward the last, but insisted that huckleberries and winter-green and birch-bark would do very well for three or four days. When asked how he could sleep in the woods alone, he said the only trouble was to keep awake, and that "it slept itself," if he only let it. The boy obstinately asserted that he liked it in the woods and had "enjoyed it first-rate." He admitted that he had got his head turned, but declared when he struck the river he understood how it was, and came back. When asked if he had heard the guns fired by the various parties that went into the woods the morning after he disappeared, he said he did, but they confused him. He would hear firing in one direction and would go toward it, after which there would be firing in another direction and he would turn toward that, and so it "mixed him all up." He had fired his gun once in reply, but, having lost his box of percussion-caps, could fire no more.

Edward and Salsify and I started on our return to the farm-house the next morning. There was an incident that amused us just as we were starting. Mr. Pinkham came to the plains to pick huckleberries, provided with a bundle of slips of paper, and on each slip was written, "Tobias Pinkham,—Lost!" He was going to tack these notices to the trees as he traveled, if he got lost, and he had a paper of small tacks in his pocket for that purpose. He agreed with some hunters that in case he should be missing they would search for him, looking out sharp for the notices. It was a very serious agreement upon Mr. Pinkham's part. He emphasized the point that he would pay the hunters for their trouble, either in money or in maple sugar. Mr. Pinkham's notices were looked upon as a great joke, and the news of them was spread abroad by us as we met the neighbors on our return journey. We reached the farm-house in time for dinner. That was three days ago. To-morrow we will return to the city.

The Court in Schoharie

On a bright, warm day the Judge and I take a train, and are whirled away from the toiling city to the rich, fertile, grassy valley of old Schoharie. It is sunk deep among the highlands, far back in a remote corner, behind the blue Catskills. The Judge has to submit to being lionized a little as we draw near the end of the journey; for a justice of the Supreme Court of the State of New York, on his way to hold a circuit in this slumberous valley, always finds himself an exceedingly great man. The little hotel at Schoharie has been dreaming of him and of the coming circuit for weeks past. The lawyers and the people from all parts of the country are waiting to do homage to the Supreme Court and to his Honor. Court-week is a prodigious affair in Schoharie: it comes but twice in the year. The fat of the land has been gathered in at the hotel to feed the Court and the multitude who come to the county-seat for justice.

When we reach the nearest railroad station and step off the cars, we discover a large, old-fashioned carriage and a pair of magnificent grays ready to receive us. The alert hotel proprietor has come all the way from his house to greet us, and his cheery voice says, "This way, Judge, with your friend, if you please."

As the grays prance along, the little valley opens to our view. It seems hardly more than a mile wide. The heights on either side are clothed with bright green woodlands, and along the highest line is a dark, rich fringe of pines. A sluggish stream winds through the middle of the valley. Just before us sleeps the hamlet, and soon we see the gleaming tin upon the church spire, and then we distinguish the court-house and other buildings. A dreamy blue in the air hangs sleepily over the landscape, imparting a sense of deep repose.

We turn a corner of the road, and here we are, right at the hotel. What a crowd of people! and what handshaking from the chief men of the country! The crowd smile a vast, substantial welcome as the Judge is ushered into the house and conducted to the best apartments. How could there be a warmer reception? The shining black faces of the servants are unctuous with good nature and the desire to please. The negroes have clung to this rich, warm spot ever since the days when the old Dutch farmers owned them as slaves. They still have a corner of the little village for their own, and upon great occasions a few of the comeliest are gathered in with the other supplies to add to the magnificence of the hotel.

After an hour comes the dinner. The lawyers have been called, and are gathered in a huddle around the outside of the dining-room door. But no one is admitted until the Judge has made his appearance. Then the group parts to the right and left, his Honor passes through, the door is opened, he goes in and is seated at the head of the table; and then the lawyers are admitted and assigned seats in the order of their supposed rank and importance.

From dinner there is an adjournment to the courthouse. The temple of justice is densely packed with people. In the little niche of a gallery high up in the wall, opposite the bench where the august court is seated, are groups of beautiful country girls and women, gazing in rapt wonder at what seems to them, doubtless, the brilliant pageant below. The lawyers also, at the bar, concede in a pleasant way, by their dress and manner, the importance of the occasion. Nate, who is, legally speaking, the pride and flower of Schoharie, appears in a bright new suit, with blue coat and gilt buttons. He is known far and wide as one of nature's noblemen. If Nate would only try, the people say, he would be a giant. As it is, he is regarded as another Daniel Webster, with a great dash of the impulsive, wayward, reckless boy in him, that too often defeats him in the far-reaching, solemn purposes of life.

The business of the court proceeds. Several petty matters are disposed of. Then the prosecuting officer of the county comes forward with a case that requires a trial by jury. Nate is counsel for the defendant. The utmost politeness prevails. It is very pleasant to see the lawyers so kind and brotherly in their treatment of each other. It is a relief to the Judge and his comrade, accustomed as they are to endure the rasping manner which is popularly supposed to be professional.

The case turns out to be merely the taking of an old coat and a turkey by a black boy from his employer. As the evidence is given, the names of localities mentioned by the witnesses are provocative of curiosity. They are also enjoyable. One has need to suffer for months from the dreary aridity of proceedings in the city courts in order to comprehend how such morsels of verbal greenness as Clover Way and Polly Hollow can refresh the legal mind. It appears that Clover Way is a nook where the clover grows in great luxuriance. Then the Judge desires to know about Polly Hollow; but it would be simply dreadful for the great Court to express publicly its curiosity upon such a trivial matter in Schoharie. A lawyer is therefore privately interviewed, and states that Polly Hollow is a clove in the mountains having the general style and description of a breech-loading gun-barrel, inasmuch as things going in at one end must go out at the other; there is not room in the clove to turn around. He says the hollow was named after Aunt Polly,—a negress who resided there for many years. He further takes occasion to point out to us a young man, who has been brought into court charged with a misdemeanor, and whose face has a curious expression of sheepishness and low cunning. That man, he informs us, is a Sloughter. He explains that the Sloughters are a band or tribe as marked and peculiar as the gypsies. They have developed into a distinct people in this valley during the present century. They are so immoral that to be seen frequenting the Sloughter settlement is a disgrace to any citizen. To call an upright man a Sloughter is a provocation that greatly mitigates an assault and battery in the eyes of a Schoharie jury.

As the case draws to a close, Nate pleads for his client with a good deal of feeling. His fine eyes melt into tears when he urges that old Schoharie may not be disgraced by having a citizen sent to the State prison.

Just as Nate is waxing eloquent, a very pretty girl, about six years of age, with brown cheeks, and a sunbonnet dangling by its string from her hand, comes in at the large open doors, walks up the aisle and into the inclosure of the bar, and, going up to Nate, pulls at his coat. Nate stops and glances downward, begs in his courtly manner to be excused for a moment, and pours out a glass of water for the little maiden from a large white pitcher on the table before him. She drinks it, and goes tripping away down the aisle again, utterly unconscious of the eyes looking at her, or of any impropriety in asking Uncle Nate at such a moment for a glass of water.

The case takes a favorable turn: the black boy escapes with only a light sentence of confinement in the county jail.

In the next proceeding we see how Cupid appears in this temple of justice.

The prosecuting officer says, "May it please the Court, we must see about this man who refuses to support his wife. It is a matter for our county authorities, of course, but there are circumstances which"—

A small, active attorney from the city springs to his feet, and, interrupting, says, "If the Court please, I appear in this case. The learned and ingenious gentleman need not explain how he gets this matter here. It is a proceeding that ought not to be tolerated anywhere. This *man* that the prosecuting officer talks about is Georgie Wilson, and he is hardly fifteen years old."

The Judge whispers with the Associate Justices of the county, who sit with him, and then says, "Where is the accused? Let him be brought forward."

"Stand up, Georgie," says his counsel.

A dandyish, sprightly little fellow, tastily dressed in handsome clothes from the city, with a bright face, light clustering curls, and blue eyes, jumps up and stands before the court.

"Won't take care of his wife, hey?" says the Judge, with an amused smile.

The girls and women in the gallery lean forward with their mouths half open and titter. A light breeze from the meadows back of the court-house comes in at an open window, and tosses Georgie's light curls very prettily.

"If your Honors please," says the prosecuting officer in a solemn voice, "this man has persistently refused and entirely neglected to support this woman, although proceedings have been taken against him."

The Court in Schoharie 111

"What woman? Where *is* his wife?—" inquires the Judge, interrupting.

A bright-eyed and prettily-dressed little girl is sent forward from the back seats, and comes and stands by Georgie. A glance at her face reveals the fact that she may be fifteen, but she is very *petite* for so many years. As they stand together, Georgie takes hold of her dress, pulls it, and whispers to her. The little beauty jerks away coquettishly, and will not look at him.

"Now, your Honors, look at these children," says the counsel for Georgie imploringly. "Is this a case to bring before the Supreme Court of the State of New York? This boy, who is well connected and respectable, has been kept in jail two weeks on this charge. His relatives, who are in good circumstances in the city, are, of course, very much annoyed by these proceedings. The boy came out here into the country one sunshiny day and was entrapped into this marriage."

The prosecuting officer replies sharply to this, and a discussion springs up which continues for ten minutes. Meanwhile, the two children are apparently making up their quarrel. Lucy begins to whisper to Georgie, and they sit down close together in two chairs handed to them by counsel. Georgie's light curls look very pretty as he nods his approval of what Lucy is saying to him. Instead of listening to the counsel, all are slyly watching the manoeuvring of this little pair of robins. Georgie makes advances, and Lucy chirps and twitters in a very bewitching way. Counsel, in whispers, compare them to the Babes in the Wood. As the prosecuting officer fulminates and thunders, the little romance in progress just in rear of his position is the real subject to which the Court directs its attention. The Judge, on the sly, is absorbed in the way Georgie manages the making up, and is observing how the little beauty reveals her inborn tendency to be "flirtatious." The curl of Lucy's lip and the flash of Georgie's eyes are much more potent than the eloquence of pugnacious attorneys.

The reconciliation seems happily completed, to the great enjoyment of the spectators, who have been feasting upon the scene, just as the wordy contest of the legal athletes closes.

"I think I will have the woman sworn, and see what the Court thinks about it," says the prosecuting officer. "I do not like to do it; but, after what has been said, I feel that I must show how this man has treated this woman. Mrs. Wilson, take the stand, if you please."

Either because she is not yet accustomed to the title "Mrs. Wilson," or more likely because she is too much absorbed with Georgie to hear the request, Lucy pays no attention to it.

"Go around there by the Judge and be sworn, Sissy," says Georgie's counsel persuasively.

Lucy hears this, and obeys, and the clerk mumbles the oath to her. At the close of the formula "You will tell the truth, the whole truth, and nothing but the truth,—kiss the book," her cherry-red lips meet the calf-skin cover of the ancient volume with a delicious smack, while she looks sweet and smiling at Georgie. Then follows her examination. The prosecuting officer persuades her into the truthful acknowledgement that she has made complaint against Georgie for not supporting her. She admits that soon after they were married, about a month ago, Georgie left her at the hotel and went away home to his mother, "and did not come back for a week," she says, pouting; but she adds that when he did come back he gave her two dollars, and paid her board at the hotel besides.

She admits also that he often asked her to walk down by the creek after they were married, and that she would not go, because she thought he had got tired of her and wanted to push her into the river. This touch of nature slightly amuses the bench and bar; but the public prosecutor assumes a horrified aspect, seeming to regard it as evidence of a very serious character.

Lucy concedes also that Georgie finally went away home to his mother, and did not come back at all; and then she had no way to pay her board, and had to leave the hotel and work out, as she used to do before she was married, and so she complained of him to the authorities.

Then Georgie's counsel takes the witness and cross-examines her. She admits that she is older than Georgie, and that she is a little French girl from Canada, and accustomed to work out. She claims that Georgie told her he was rich and that she could live like a lady at the hotel. She says she would not have cared for not having much, if he had only told her the truth, for she was quite able to take care of herself, she thanks fortune; but she was angry at Georgie for acting so; but now they have made it up, and she would like to have him set at liberty, if they please.

Lucy comes down from the stand and sits by Georgie again, and he takes her hands, and they look wonderingly into each other's faces, as children do.

"Now, your Honors," says Georgie's counsel, "you must see how this is. This little girl, who is older than she appears, and was a servant, has caught this boy and privately married him. He is of good family: he could not take this girl home with him, probably because his mother would not want her there. Let this proceeding stop, and Georgie and his friends will make the best of it. He is married to the girl, and they will try to take care of her in some way. I am authorized by them to say this to the Court."

The Court takes a lenient view of the case. Georgie is directed to stand up, and the Judge delivers a lecture to him in regard to his duties as a husband. Georgie is informed that it is perhaps unfortunate for him that he has married "this girl" (the little beauty's cheeks burn at this), but that he must nevertheless take care of her. He is permitted to go at large for the time being without punishment; but he must remember that he is on probation and under the watchful eyes of the officers of the law.

Georgie and Lucy, happy and side by side, go chirpingly out of the court-room, and many kind wishes and the mirth of the happy hour go with them.

Other cases are presented and disposed of, until the business of the day is closed. It is said that to-morrow a breach of promise case will come on for trial.

In the evening there is a pleasant walk along the one street of the town, and a chat in our rooms with the lawyers. We are reminded by them of the fact that one of the Associate Justices, coming from a remote corner of the county where the people still continue to vote for General Jackson, presented himself with his boots unblacked. It is remarked also that he wore no cravat, and not even a paper collar, as he sat in dignity upon the bench with the Judge of the Supreme Court of the State. We are informed that he has been mischievously notified that a committee of the Democratic party will be appointed to consider the matter. It is said that we will see the result in the morning.

We retire to rest. The fragrance of grasses and clover is wafted in at our open windows. Across the meadows back of the hotel, in a grove, we see lights flitting here and there, and the sound of far-off tinkling music is borne to our ears. It is the negro population enjoying a dance, as part of the festivities of the week.

The lawyers of Schoharie County are found to be wonderfully pleasant fellows. The Judge and his comrade discover that these gentlemen sleep but little. It is a habit with them to spend their nights in the valley upon great occasions in hilarity and good fellowship. The Judge and his comrade virtuously keep aloof from these nightly carousings. But how can this sanctimonious pair, with their faces pale and worn with city life, foul air, and excitement, hint to these strong, healthy, vigorous gentlemen that nightly rejoicing is not calculated to promote health? Their ancient owlish custom has its poetic side. It is pleasant for a cheerful person to awake in the night and faintly hear the deep voice of a distinguished lawyer pronouncing a solemn discourse in some remote room of the hotel. The voices of many members of the bar, and of the black servants, and a far-off clapping of hands, are occasionally distinguished, as the orator bears down with mock solemnity upon the vanity of earth and the folly of all human affairs. When the oration is completed, the long-drawn notes of "Old Hundred" steal solemnly along the dark halls of the hotel to the ears of the lodgers. Then all is quiet, and the Schoharie County Bar retires to rest.

Next morning at breakfast we are informed that the ceremonies of a grand initiation of a new member into the strange mysteries of the "Schoharie Circle" were performed at some hour of the night.

After breakfast we have an hour before court-time. Shall the Sheriff take us for a ride, or will we have Esquire John to show us the curiosities of the place? We elect to have John, and soon he comes to the hotel. He is a robust, medium-sized man, a quaint scholar, a genuine lover of nature, and has the quick step and merry eye of a boy. He tells us that he had part in the grand initiation we overheard in the night. When we compliment him upon his vigorous health, he suggests that it may be due to the fact that he eats a meal of delicious oysters every night at eleven o'clock.

John takes us first half a mile away through the green fields back of the hotel, up to a shelf or natural terrace projecting from the steep hill-side that walls in the valley. Here we find ourselves among the white marble slabs of a cemetery; and John points out the graves where the German forefathers of the hamlet sleep. He tells us that some of the Palatines came across the country from the Hudson in 1710 and discovered this beautiful valley, and in 1713 they came here and settled. Then he traces the history of monumental art in the valley, pointing out the old gray limestone cemetery slabs of ancient date with their queer carvings, and then the lighter sandstone, and at length the monumental marble. He calls our attention also to the cedar-trees and the arbor vitæ in the cemetery grounds. Forty years ago, he tells us, he planted these trees with his own hands, and they are his gift to the people.

John points out a place hard by where the first settlers erected their church in 1750. All their names, he assures us, were carved upon the foundation-stones of the sacred edifice.

From the cemetery John takes us higher up the hillside to a rocky place and a stone-quarry. Here he points out abrasions and long scratches in the surface of the polished rock. These, he explains, are glacier-marks. He demonstrates with the fine enthusiasm of a true lover of science where the icy stream must have flowed in the dim and faded centuries of an unknown past. He pictures very vividly the glacier in its grinding progress over the rock when the Catskills were as high as the Alps and Schoharie a mass of ice. He paints with glowing words an unknown world. The Judge politely asks him how he knows all that he describes to be true. John points triumphantly to the scratches in the rock, and his eloquence is renewed with tenfold fervor. He overwhelms our doubts, and we are convinced.

Then he calls attention to the features of the valley as it now exists. Across upon the other side we discern terraces which he tells us are graperies. The view, he assures us, is somewhat like what may be seen along the Rhine or in Switzerland. He has never been to those distant places, but travelers have declared to him that in his native valley he has in miniature the scenery of the world. He is satisfied with this, and has no desire to leave his home, until his friends shall bear him to his last rest beneath the cedars and the arbor vitæ upon the hill-side.

Returning toward the hotel, we pass near the present church edifice, built in 1776. The date is seen in huge iron figures upon the tower. John tells us that the stones that were the foundation of the church first erected by the settlers were taken out and brought down and used for the foundation of this modern structure.

We go and examine the foundation, and find carved in rude German letters the names of the forefathers.

John tells us that the stone church, a mile away down the valley, was once used as a fort, and that a cannon-ball fired in time of war is embedded in the tower. He enlarges upon the history of the valley, rendering it apparent that not only the scenery but the history of the world is to be found in miniature in Schoharie. Even the emancipation experiment has been tested there by fifty years of trial. He is bound to add that the two hundred negroes in Schoharie retain their prodigal and shiftless habits to this day. He does not think any important change has been effected in their prospects or character.

John has one more curiosity to show us. We will go with him to a little building which he calls his office, where he has gathered and arranged the fossils and minerals and curious historical relics of the region. He presents for our inspection the ancient vane that adorned the spire of the church built by the early settlers. This vane is of iron, and in the form of a crowing cock, with magnificent flowing tail-feathers. John assures us that this cock crowed for many years upon the banks of the Rhine before the Palatines brought it with them to Schoharie.

While we are looking, the court-house bell surprises us, and we hasten away. Reaching the court-room, we find the crowd even denser than on the previous day. A little formal business is first transacted. A sly glance reveals that the Associate Justice has been frightened into a paper collar, but resists other innovations. He is making his stand upon the boots: they remain unblackened and brown and rusty.

The formal matters having been disposed of, the breach of promise case is taken up. The defendant is a stout, honest-faced countryman. His lawyer is the attorney from the city. It seems that the affair occurred years ago, when the defendant was a bachelor. A neighborhood quarrel has now revived it. The sharp points are brought out upon the cross-examination.

It hardly seems worth while to take so deep an interest in so simple a matter; but there we all are,—the court, the bar, the jury, and the spectators, all drinking in with great eagerness Miss Sallie Brown's story as she is persecuted by the attorney from the city.

"Do you swear that he promised to marry you, Sallie?" asks the counsel cross-examining.

"Yes, I do," says Sallie sharply.

"How old are you, Sallie?" continues her inquisitor.

"I don't know what that has to do with it," protests the witness; "but I would just as soon tell you. I am forty-six; but I was only forty-two when he promised to marry me, and he was forty-four."

"Now, Miss Sallie," says the counsel, "do you really mean to swear that John entangled your maiden affections and plighted his troth to you, after an acquaintance of only three weeks, having seen you but twice, he being a steady blacksmith, and you a country maiden of forty-two summers?—do you mean that, now, Sallie?"

"Yes, I do *mean* it," responds the irate spinster.

"How did he say it? What did he say first?" inquires the lawyer.

"Why, the first time when he went away he asked me to remember him in my prayers; and I told him I would."

"Did you do it?" demands the lawyer, interrupting.

"Certainly I did," says the witness, "and I always have. And the next time he came we were in the parlor, and he said, 'Sallie, will you have me?' and he took his hand into mine, and I said, 'Yes;' and he said he hoped I would never be sorry, and I said I never would if he did as he agreed to."

"Did he squeeze your hand?" asks the counsel.

"Not enough to hurt it, I guess," responds the maiden snappishly.

"Did he press your hand in a manner that indicated peculiar affection for yourself?" inquires the Judge, with impressive blandness and evident relish.

"Oh, yes, certainly," says the maiden sweetly.

"And," continues the Judge, smiling and looking squarely into the blue eyes of the witness, "did he use—ah—terms of endearment to you, Miss Sallie?"

"He only said what I have told you," replies the lady, in a soft voice.

"Ahem!" says the Judge, with a disappointed air, as he turns away and makes a note upon his papers.

"And did he kiss you?" asks the counsel roughly.

"Yes, he did kiss me, if you are so anxious to know," jerks out the injured female.

"Do I understand you to testify," says the Judge, brightening up, "that he pressed your hand caressingly and kissed you?"

"Yes, sir," answers the maiden, with a grateful glance.

"And," continues the Judge slowly, dwelling with evident pleasure upon the words, "did he by his manner express endearment and attachment and peculiar affection,—that is, a sentiment of especial and endearing regard for you,—as he caressingly pressed your hand?"

"Yes, sir," replies the lady softly, dropping her eyelids as she meets the keen, searching gaze of his Honor.

"Where did he kiss you?—on your cheek or your lips?" now resumes her tormentor.

Sallie thinks she is badgered, and remains silent.

"Please tell us where he kissed you, Miss Sallie," says the Judge kindly.

"It was on my lips, sir," says the lady, in a very low voice, to the Judge.

"She says it was on her lips," announces the Judge, with an air of great satisfaction, as he turns to his papers and makes a note of the fact.

"Now, perhaps you will tell me how many times he kissed you," says the tormentor.

"He kissed me once, and that is enough for you to know," responds the indignant woman.

"When was that?" continues the interrogator.

"When he went away," replies the witness.

"Do I understand you," says the Judge apprehensively, "to say that he did not kiss you at the time he pressed your hand endearingly and affectionately and asked you if you would have him?"

"It was not then," replies the witness; "but it was when he went away."

"And," says the Judge anxiously, "did he kiss you only once?"

"That was all," replied the witness.

And the Judge, apparently disconcerted and unhappy, turns to his papers and makes a note, which he regards for a moment with great gravity.

"And na-ow," says the tormentor, with a provoking drawl, "to sum up, you mean to swear, do you, that, after three weeks' acquaintance, Swackhammer John here won the innocent, untried, and maiden affection of your too susceptible heart, and, having squeezed your hand, promised to marry you, and then, trying the taste of one kiss upon your virgin lips, *scud* for home, and never came back? Is that it, Miss Brown?"

"I did not come here to be insulted," retorts the jilted female angrily; and she flounces off the witness-stand, to the great amusement of the spectators.

After further proceedings it comes to John's turn to tell his side of the story. He "swears" with the same energetic force with which he is accustomed to wield the sledge-hammer in the shop. He declares, with a whack of his great fist upon his knee, that he never did promise to marry Sallie,—no, never, so help him his Maker, he never did! He admits that he was introduced to her by friends when he was looking for a wife, and that he called upon her twice, as she says.

"And did you," says the Judge, with a slow, delicious utterance of every syllable, "did you at any time press her hand caressingly in an affectionate and endearing manner, or indicate feelings of peculiar interest or attachment?"

"No, your Honor, I did not," says John. "I looked her over by lamplight and then by daylight, and I see it did n't take; and I said as much to the folks as introduced me. She skeered me some, she did, the second time I called. She turned on me sudden, after we had set a few minutes, and said, sez she, 'Mr. Poget, what is your intentions?' It kind of took my breath away."

"And what did you answer?" inquires the counsel.

"I was all struck of a heap for a while," says the witness; "but when I got my wind ag'in, I asked her if I could have two weeks to consider it, and she said I might; and so then I comed away."

"And did you kiss her?" inquires the Judge.

"No, I never did in my life, so help me my Maker!" with a great whack of the fist upon his knee again.

"Did you go to tell her what your intentions were, at the close of the two weeks?" asks the counsel.

"I tried to tell her," says John, "but she dodged. She sent me word she would not be at home. But I was bound to keep my appointment, and I walked over there on time, square."

"And how far was it?" says the counsel.

"Better than four mile," replies the witness.

"As I was sayin', I walked over there, and she was not there. I found her father there, and talked to him awhile, and then went home. I saw Sallie the next week, at the store, and I told her I had my mind made up not to give up my bachelorship quite yet, and I did not want to marry her. She cried, and I told her not to feel bad, and I left her; and she and I never spoke no more."

The Judge, in charging the jury, says, "And although, gentlemen, this proceeding, even upon the plaintiff's own statement, is not as warm and ardent as our experience might lead us to expect, and although there is a frigidity about it which does not perhaps fully satisfy the mind, yet, if you believe this man did gently press this woman's hand in a manner denoting and intended to denote peculiar affection, and if they did mutually promise marriage, that promise is binding."

As the jury go out, John's counsel smilingly remarks that the Court evidently regards this as an interesting case. A pleasant ripple of merriment testifies that the shot tells, and a pretty blush upon the noble, time-worn face of his Honor reveals the still youthful susceptibility of his heart.

The jury are out all night. In the mean time, John and his family are sleepless and trembling through the lone night watches. The comedy in the court-room has for them its terrors. Their little shop and farm may be swept from them by a verdict awarding damages to Sallie.

In the morning, the court-room is again crowded. It is whispered that the jury have agreed, and soon they are brought in. John sits with his counsel, trembling and fearing.

The clerk of the court says to the jury, "Gentlemen, have you agreed upon your verdict?"

The foreman rises, and replies, "We have agreed."

"How do you find?" asks the clerk.

"For the defendant," replies the foreman.

John's head goes down upon his hands, and he buries his face between his knees. The sudden joy and relief is too much for him. His great shoulders heave and sway in his efforts to repress his sobs. The counsel laugh and jog him and tell him to "hold up," they want to speak to him.

John rises to his feet with a great swing and a jerk designed to throw his long hair back from his red, excited face, which is seen to be all wet with tears, and, grabbing his hat, he rushes from the court-room.

Ten minutes later, the counsel find him and his family at the hotel where they have put up, crying and laughing and hugging each other in the excess of their great joy. The avalanche of an angry woman's vengeance, which has threatened them for a year past in the shape of this lawsuit, can never crush them now, and they look into a future without a cloud.

A day later, the court adjourns *sine die.* The crowd of people in wagons and on foot make their way out of town, and the hamlet seems almost deserted. The carriage and the grays are brought to the door, and we prepare to leave Schoharie. A group of lawyers and their friends gather around and give us each the final handshake and kind words at parting. We take our places in the carriage, and the landlord sits with the driver to escort us to the depot. He tells us confidentially that it has been a magnificent court; that he has not slept two hours during the entire week; that the strain has been tremendous, but that he has made seven hundred dollars.

We arrive at the depot, and soon the train comes thundering along and puffs and shrieks and awakens all the echoes of the highlands. It seems like a brazen and impudent affront offered to the slumbering spirits of the valley. The train pauses a moment: we secure seats, and are whirled away toward the dust and the noise and toil of the city. As we look backward through the car-window and catch a flying glimpse of the blue, fading valley, we sigh, and say that our summer court at Schoharie is over.

Tompkins

He was a small, wiry man, about forty years of age, with a bright young face, dark eyes, and iron-gray hair. We were reclining in a field, under a clump of pines, on a height overlooking Lake Champlain. Near by were the dull-red brick buildings of the University of Vermont. Burlington, blooming with flowers and embowered in trees, sloped away below us. Beyond the town, the lake, a broad plain of liquid blue, slept in the June sunshine, and in the farther distance towered the picturesque Adirondacks.

"It is certainly true," said Tompkins, turning upon his side so as to face me, and propping his head with his hand, while his elbow rested on the ground. "Don't you remember, I used to insist that they were peculiar, when we were here in college?"

I remembered it very distinctly, and so informed my old classmate.

"I always said," he continued, "that I could not do my best in New England, because there is no sentiment in the atmosphere, and the people are so peculiar."

"You have been living in Chicago?" I remarked inquiringly.

"That has been my residence ever since we were graduated; that is, for about seventeen years," he replied.

"You are in business there, I believe?" I questioned.

Tompkins admitted that he was, but did not name the particular line.

"Halloo!" he suddenly called out, rising to his feet, and looking toward the little brown road near us. I looked in the same direction, and saw a plainly dressed elderly couple on foot, apparently out for a walk. Tompkins went hastily toward them, helped the lady over the fence, the gentleman following, and a moment later I was introduced to Mr. and Mrs. Pember, of Chicago.

Tompkins gathered some large stones, pulled a board off the fence in rather a reckless manner, and fixed a seat for the couple where they could lean against a tree. When they were provided for, I reclined again, but Tompkins stood before us, talking and gesticulating.

"This," said he, "is the identical place, Mrs. Pember. Here you can see the beauties I have so often described. Before you are the town and the lake, and beyond them the mountains of Northern New York; and (if you will please to turn your head) that great blue wall behind you, twenty miles away, is composed of the highest mountains in Vermont. The mountains in front of you are the Adirondacks, and those behind you are the Green Mountains. You are at the central point of this magnificent Champlain Valley; and you are comfortably seated here beneath the shade, on this the loveliest day of summer. Dear friends, I congratulate you," and Tompkins shook hands with Mr. and Mrs. Pember.

"And there, Timothy," observed the old gentleman, pointing at the University buildings with his cane, "is actually where you went to college."

"It was in those memorable and classic halls, as my classmate here can testify," replied Tompkins. "And here we roamed in 'Academus' sacred shade,' and a good deal beyond it. We went fishing and boating during term time, and made long trips to the mountains in the vacations. In the mean time, this wonderful valley was photographed upon the white and spotless sensorium of my youthful soul."

"Going, going, going!" cried Mrs. Pember, with a light, rippling laugh, glancing at me. "That is the way I stop Mr. Tompkins when he gets too flowery."

Tompkins looked at me and reddened. "I own up," he remarked, "I am an auctioneer in Chicago."

I hastened to say that I felt sure he was a good one, and added, in the kindest way I could, that I had just been wondering how he had become such a good talker.

"Is it a good deal of a come-down?" asked Tompkins, with a mixture of frankness and embarrassment.

I replied that the world was not what we had imagined in our college days, and that the calling of an auctioneer was honorable.

A general conversation followed, in the course of which it appeared that Tompkins had boarded at the home of the Pembers for several years. They evidently looked upon him almost as their own son. They were traveling with him during his summer rest.

"This is a queer world," observed Tompkins, dropping down beside me, and lying flat on his back, with his hands under his head. "I came to college from a back neighborhood over in York State, and up to the day I was graduated, and for a long time afterward, I thought I must be President of the United States, or a Presbyterian minister, or a great poet, or something remarkable, and here I am an auctioneer."

Occasional remarks were made by the rest of us for a while, but soon the talking was mainly done by Tompkins.

Said he, "Since I was graduated, I never was back here but once before, and that was four years ago next August. I was traveling this way then, and reached here Saturday evening. I was in the pork business at that time, as a clerk, and had to stop off here to see a man for the firm. I put up at the best hotel, feeling as comfortable and indifferent as I ever did in my life. There was not the shadow of an idea in my mind of what was going to happen. On Sunday morning I walked about town, and it began to come down on me."

"What, the town?" asked Mrs. Pember.

"No; the strangest and most unaccountable feeling I ever had in my life," answered Tompkins. "It was thirteen years since I had said good-by to college. It had long ago become apparent to me that the ideas with which I had graduated were visionary and impracticable. I comprehended that the college professors were not the great men I had once thought them, and that a college president was merely a human being. I had been hardened by fighting my way, as a friendless young man has to do in a great city. As the confidential clerk of a large pork house in Chicago, I felt equal to the 'next man,' whoever he might be. If a professor had met me as I got off the cars here Saturday night, it would have been easy for me to snub him. But Sunday morning, as familiar objects began to appear in the course of my walk, the strange feeling of which I have spoken came over me. It was the feeling of old times. The white clouds, the blue lake, this wonderful scenery, thrilled me, and called back the college dreams."

As he spoke, my old classmate's voice trembled.

"You may remember that I used to like Horace and Virgil and Homer," he remarked, sitting up, crossing his feet tailor-fashion, and looking appealingly at me.

I replied, enthusiastically and truly, that he had been one of our best lovers of the poets.

"Well," continued Tompkins, "that Sunday morning those things began to come back to me. It was n't exactly delightful. My old ambition to do something great in the world awoke as if from a long sleep. As I prolonged my walk the old associations grew stronger. When I came near the college buildings it seemed as if I still belonged here. The hopes of an ideal career were before me as bright as ever. The grand things I was going to do, the volumes of poems and other writings by Tompkins, and his marvelous successes were as clear as day. In short, the whole thing was conjured up as if it were a picture, just as it used to be when I was a student in college, and it was too much for me."

Tompkins seemed to be getting a little hoarse, and his frank face was very serious.

"Timothy," suggested Mr. Pember, "may be you could tell us what that big rock is, out in the lake."

"Why, father, don't you remember? That is rock Dunder," said Mrs. Pember.

"I guess it is," said the old gentleman, musingly.

"Well," resumed Tompkins, "as I was saying, on one side were Homer and Virgil and Horace and Tompkins, and on the other was pork. I cannot explain it, but somehow there it was. The two pictures, thirteen years apart, were brought so close together that they touched. It was something I do not pretend to understand. Managing to get by the college buildings, I came up to this spot where we are now. You will infer that my eyes watered badly, and to tell the truth they did. Of course it is all very well," explained Tompkins, uncrossing his legs, turning upon his side, and propping his head on his hand again,— "of course it is all very well to rake down the college, and say *Alma Mater* does n't amount to anything. The boys all do it, and they believe what they say for the first five or six years after they leave here. But we may as well understand that if we know how to slight the old lady, and don't go to see her for a dozen years, she knows how to punish. She had me across her knee, that Sunday morning, in a way that I would have thought impossible. After an hour I controlled myself, and went back to the hotel. I brushed my clothes, and started for church, with a lump in my throat all the while. My trim business suit did n't seem so neat and nobby as usual. The two pictures, the one of the poets and the other of pork, were in my mind. I shied along the sidewalk in a nervous condition, and reaching the church without being recognized managed to get a seat near the door. Could I believe my senses? I knew that I was changed, probably past all recognition, but around me I saw the faces of my Burlington friends exactly as they had been thirteen years before. I did not understand then, as I do now, that a young man in business in Chicago will become gray-headed in ten years, though he might have lived a quiet life in Vermont for a quarter of a century, without changing a hair."

"It is the same with horses," suggested Mr. Pember. "Six years on a horse-car in New York about uses up an average horse, though he would have been good for fifteen years on a farm."

"Exactly," said Tompkins. "You can imagine how I felt that Sunday, with my hair half whitewashed."

"You know I always said you might have begun coloring your hair, Timothy," said Mrs. Pember kindly.

"Yes," replied Tompkins, with an uneasy glance at me; "but I did n't do it. There was one thing in the church there, that morning, that I shall never have a better chance to tell of, and I am going to tell it now, while you are here."

This last sentence was addressed to me, and my old classmate uttered the words with a gentleness and frankness that brought back my best recollections of him in our college days, when he was "little Tompkins," the warmest-hearted fellow in our class.

"Do you remember Lucy Cary?" he asked.

I replied that I did, very well indeed; and the picture of a youthful face, of Madonna-like beauty, came out with strange distinctness from the memories of the past, as I said it.

"Well, I saw Lucy there," continued Tompkins, "singing in the choir in church, looking just as she did in the long-ago days when we used to serenade her. I am willing to tell you about it."

Tompkins said this in such a confiding manner that I instinctively moved toward him and took hold of his hand.

"All right, classmate," he said, sitting up, and looking me in the eyes in a peculiarly winning way that had won us all when he was in college.

"Why, boys!" exclaimed Mrs. Pember, with her light laugh.

Tompkins found a large stone, put it against a tree, and sat down on it, while I reclined at his feet. He said,—

"You have asked me, Mrs. Pember, very often, about the people up here, and now I will tell you about some of them. Do you notice that mountain away beyond the lake, in behind the others, so that you can see only the top, which is shaped like a pyramid? That is old Whiteface, and it is more than forty miles from here. It used to be understood that there was nothing whatever over there except woods and rocks and bears and John Brown. But the truth is, right at the foot of the mountain, in the valley on this side, there is a little village called Wilmington, and it is the centre of the world. Lucy Cary and I were born there. It was not much of a village then, and it is about the same now. There was no church and no store, and no hotel, in my time; there were only half a dozen dwelling-houses, and a blacksmith shop, and a man who made shoes. Lucy lived in the house next to ours. Her father was the man who made shoes. Lucy and I picked berries and rambled about with Rover, the dog, from the time we were little. Of course you will naturally think there is something romantic coming, but there is not. We were just a couple of children playing together; and we studied together as we grew older. They made a great deal of studying and schooling over there. They had almost as much respect for learning then in Wilmington as they have now among the White Mountains, where they will not allow any waiters at the hotels who cannot talk Greek.

"It was quite an affair when Lucy and I left Wilmington and came to Burlington. The departure of two inhabitants was a loss to the town. It was not equal to the Chicago fire, but it was an important event. I went to college, and Lucy came over the lake to work in a woolen factory. *There* is where she worked," pointing to the beautiful little village of Winooski, a mile away behind us, in the green valley of Onion River.

"And she had to work there for a living, while you went to college?" asked Mrs. Pember.

"That was it," said Tompkins. "We used to serenade her sometimes, with the rest; but she seemed to think it was not exactly the right thing for a poor factory girl, and so we gave it up. I used to see her occasionally, but somehow there grew up a distance between us."

"How was that?" inquired Mrs. Pember.

"Well, to tell the truth," answered Tompkins, "I think my college ideas had too much to do with it. I did not see it at the time, but it has come over me lately. When a young chap gets his head full of new ideas, he is very likely to forget the old ones."

"You did not mean to do wrong, I am sure," said Mrs. Pember.

"The excuse I have," continued Tompkins, "is that I had to work and scrimp and suffer so myself, to get along and pay my way, that I hardly thought of anything except my studies and how to meet my expenses. Then there was that dream of doing some great thing in the world. I taught the district school in Wilmington three months during my Sophomore year to get money to go on with, and I think that helped to make me ambitious. It was the sincere conviction of the neighborhood over there that I would be president of the college or of the United States. I do not think they would have conceded that there was much difference in the two positions. I felt that I would be disgraced if I did not meet their expectations. By one of those coincidences which seemed to follow our fortunes, Lucy made a long visit home when I was teaching in Wilmington. She was one of my pupils. She was a quiet little lady, hardly spoke a loud word, that I remember, all winter."

"Did you try to talk to her, Timothy?" asked Mrs. Pember.

"I do not claim that I did," answered Tompkins. "I was studying hard to keep up with my class, and that was the reason. But I wish I had paid more attention to Lucy Cary that winter. I would not have you think there was anything particular between Lucy and me. It was not that."

"We will think just what we please," interrupted Mrs. Pember, in a serious tone.

"Well," continued the narrator, "it would be absurd to suppose there was any such thing."

There was a long pause. "You had better tell the rest of the story, Timothy," said the old gentleman, persuasively.

"Yes, I will," responded Tompkins. "After I came back to college I got along better than before I had taught. The money I received for teaching helped me, and another thing aided me. The folks in Wilmington found out how a poor young man works to get through college. Some of us used to live on a dollar a week apiece, and board ourselves in our rooms, down there in the buildings; and we were doing the hardest kind of studying at the same time. We would often club together, one doing the cooking for five or six. The cook would get off without paying. It was one of the most delightful things in the world to see a tall young man in a calico dressing-gown come out on the green, where we would be playing football, and make the motions of beating an imaginary gong for dinner. In order to appreciate it, you need to work hard and play hard and live on the slimmest kind of New England fare. But there is one thing even better than that. To experience the most exquisite delight ever known by a Burlington student, you ought to have an uncle Jason. While I was teaching in Wilmington, my uncle Jason, from North Elba, which was close by, came there. When he found out what an important man I was, and how I was fighting my way, he sympathized wonderfully. He was not on good terms at our house, but he called at my school, and almost cried over me. He was not a man of much learning, but he looked upon those who were educated as a superior order of beings. I was regarded in the neighborhood as a sort of martyr to science, a genius who was working himself to death. I was the only public man ever produced by the settlement up to that date. It was part of the religion of the place to look upon me as something unusual, and uncle Jason shared the general feeling. I could see, as he sat there in the school-house observing the school, that he was very proud of me. Before leaving, he called me into the entry and gave me a two-dollar bill. It was generous, for he was a poor man, and had his wife and children to support. It brought the tears to my eyes when he handed me the money, and told me I was the flower of the family and the pride of the settlement. I felt as if I would rather die than fail of fulfilling the expectations of my friends. There was great delight in it, and it was an inexpressible joy to know that my relatives and the neighbors cared so much for me.

"To comprehend this thing fully, Mrs. Pember, you ought to be in college, and when you are getting hard up, and see no way but to leave, get letters, as I did from uncle Jason, with five or six dollars at a time in them. Such a trifle would carry you through to the end of the term, and save your standing in the class. If you were a Burlington college boy, while you might be willing to depart this life in an honorable manner, you would not be willing to lose your mark and standing as a student. You would regard the consequences of such a disaster as very damaging to your character, and certain to remain with you forever.

"I may as well say, while it is on my mind, that I *do* think this matter of education is a little overdone in this part of the country. A young man is not the centre of the universe merely because he is a college student, or a graduate, and it is not worth while to scare him with any such idea. The only way he can meet the expectation of his friends, under such circumstances, is to get run over accidentally by the cars. That completes his martyrdom, and affords his folks an opportunity to boast of what he would have been if he had lived."

"Tell us more about Lucy," said Mrs. Pember.

"Yes, certainly," replied Tompkins. "Lucy had a wonderful idea of poetry and writing. It is really alarming to a stranger to see the feeling there is up here in that way. The impression prevails generally that a writer is superior to all other people on earth. I remember to have heard that one of our class, a year after we were graduated, started a newspaper back here about ten miles, on the bank of the Onion River. He might just as well have started it under a sage bush out on the alkali plains. He gave it some queer Greek name, and I heard that the publication was first semi-weekly, then weekly, and then very weakly indeed, until it came to a full stop at the end of six months. It would have been ridiculous anywhere else; but being an attempt at literature, I suppose it was looked upon here as respectable."

"And did you use to write poetry?" queried Mrs. Pember.

"Not to any dangerous extent," replied Tompkins. "I do not deny that I tried while in college, but I reformed when I went West. I think uncle Jason always had an idea that it might be better for me to be Daniel Webster. He stood by me after I left college, and for three years I continued to get those letters, with five or six dollars at a time in them. They kept me from actual suffering sometimes, before I got down off my stilts, and went to work, like an honest man, in the pork business."

"I thought you were going to tell us something about that girl," suggested Mrs. Pember.

"Yes, I was," rejoined Tompkins. "When I saw Lucy here, four years ago, in the gallery with the singers, I felt as if it would be impossible for me to face her and talk with her. She would not have known me, for one thing. When I was a brown-haired boy, making poetry and being a martyr, and doing serenading, and living on codfish and crackers and soup, I could meet Lucy with a grand air that made her shudder; but, as I sat there in church, gray and worn, I dreaded to catch her eye, or have her see me. Although there was not three years' difference in our ages, yet it seemed to me that I was very old, while she was still blooming. Then there was the feeling that I had not become a great poet, or orator, or anything really worth while. On the contrary, I was just nobody. It seemed like attending my own funeral. I felt disgraced. Of course it was not all true. I had been a good, square, honest, hard-working man."

"Yes, you had indeed, Timothy," assented Mrs. Pember, with an emphatic nod.

"Yes indeed, I had," repeated Tompkins, his chin quivering. "It was not the thing for a fair-minded man to think so poorly of himself; but I was alone, and the old associations and the solemn services were very impressive. There was Lucy in the choir; she always could sing like a nightingale. When I heard her voice again, it overcame me. I did not hear much of the sermon. I think it was something about temptation and the suggestions of the evil one; but I am not sure, for I had my head down on the back of the pew in front of me most of the time. I had to fight desperately to control my feelings. One minute I would think that as soon as the services closed I would rush around and shake hands with my old acquaintances, and the next minute would be doing my best to swallow the lump in my throat. It was as tough a sixty minutes as I ever passed. But finally the services were ended. I felt that it was plainly my duty to stop in the porch and claim the recognition of my friends. I did pause, and try for a few seconds to collect myself; but the lump grew bigger and choked me, while the tears *would* flow. Besides that, as the adversary just then, in the meanest possible manner, suggested to my soul, there was that pork. I knew I would have to tell of it if I stopped. But I did not stop; I retreated. When I reached my room in the hotel I felt a longing to get out of town. Fortunately, I could not leave on Sunday. So in the afternoon I sat with the landlord on his broad front platform, or piazza. It was not the person who keeps the place now, but one of the oldest inhabitants, who knew all about the Burlington people. He guessed that I was a college boy; he thought he remembered something about my appearance. I did not mind talking freely with a landlord, for hotels and boardinghouses had been my home in Chicago. I had always been a single man, just as I am to this day. This landlord was a good-hearted old chap, and it was pleasant to talk with him. While we were sitting there, who should come along the street but Lucy, with a book in her hand. She was on the opposite sidewalk, and did not look up. She would not look at a hotel on Sunday. I asked the landlord about her, and he told me all there was to tell. She was living in one end of a little wooden cottage over toward Winooski, another factory woman occupying the other part of the house. They made a home together. The landlord said Lucy was an excellent woman, and might have married one of the overseers in the factory any time she chose for years back, but that she preferred a single life.

"When I got back to Chicago I kept thinking about Lucy Cary. The old times when we used to live in Wilmington came back to my mind. The truth of it was, I was getting along a little, at last, in Chicago in the way of property, and I found myself all the while planning how I could have Lucy Cary near me."

"Did you want to marry her, Timothy?" inquired Mrs. Pember.

"It was not that," he replied: "but I wanted to become acquainted with her again. I knew she was the best girl I had ever seen. She always was just as good and pious as anybody could be. We were like brother and sister, almost, when young; and when I thought of home and my folks and old Wilmington and the college days, somehow Lucy was the centre of it all. In fact, almost everything else was gone. My folks were scattered, and Lucy and uncle Jason were nearly the only persons up this way that I could lay claim to. There is a kind of lonesome streak comes over a man when he has been grinding away in a great city for a good many years, and comes back to the old places, and sees them so fresh and green and quiet, and he can't get over it. He will cling to anything that belongs to old times. I was strongly influenced to write to Lucy, but finally I did not. I determined that I would get all I could for two or three years, and then I would come here and face things. I would get something comfortable, and would have a place I could call my own in Chicago. Then, when I had it fixed, I would come and see uncle Jason and Lucy, and stand the racket. Of course it was nonsense to feel shy, but it seemed to me that I could not say a word until I had something to brag of. They knew, in a general kind of way, that I was in Chicago, dealing in pork, or doing auctioneering or something, and that was as much humiliation as I could endure. To be sure, it was nothing to be ashamed of, for I had been an honest, faithful man; but to come back to my friends empty-handed, without money or fame, and gray-headed at that, was more than I could stand. If I had *had* anything or *been* anything, just to take the edge off, I could have managed it. As it was, I looked ahead and worked. If any man in Chicago has tried and planned and toiled during the last three years, I am that man. There has been a picture before my mind of a pleasant home there."

"And have you calculated to marry Lucy Cary?" inquired Mrs. Pember, in an eager voice.

"Perhaps it was not just in that way I thought of it," replied the narrator, very seriously. "You know I told you that the landlord said she preferred a single life."

"Timothy Tompkins," exclaimed the old lady apprehensively, "don't deny it,—don't! Think how dreadfully you will feel if you know you have told a lie!"

"It is nothing to be ashamed of, Timothy," said Mr. Pember, in a kind and sympathetic voice.

"If you put it in that way," answered my old classmate, in strangely mournful tones, "all I can say is, there was never anything between us,—nothing at all."

"And did you come here this time to see her?" inquired Mrs. Pember, almost starting from her seat, and with the thrill of a sudden guess in her voice.

"I suppose it was as much that as anything," replied Tompkins doggedly, looking down, and poking with a short stick in the ground at his feet.

"And that is what has made you act so queer," mused Mrs. Pember. "Have you seen her?"

"Let *him* tell the story, Caroline," urged the old gentleman peevishly.

Tompkins looked gloomily out upon the lake and the broad landscape for a few moments; and then, resuming his narrative, said,—

"As I was saying, I have worked hard, and have got a nice little pile. I am worth thirty-five thousand dollars. When I made up my mind to come East this summer, the money to pay uncle Jason for what he had done was all ready. It made me choke to think how long I had let it run. I figured it up as near as I could,—the two hundred that came to me in college, and the two hundred after that; and I put in the simple interest at seven per cent., according to the York State law, which brought the sum total up to nearly nine hundred; and to fix it all right I made it an even thousand dollars. Then I bought a new buckskin bag, and went to a bank in Chicago and got the money all in gold. I knew that would please uncle Jason. He once talked of going to California to dig. I suppose he had never seen a pile of the real yellow coin in his life. I wrote to him that I was to be in Burlington, and that I would be ever so glad if he would come over and see me. I met him yesterday afternoon, as he got off the boat, down at the steamboat landing. He knew me, and I knew him, although we were both changed a good deal. After we had talked a little, and got used to each other, I took him up to my room in the hotel. I was in a hurry to get at the business part of my visit with him first; for it seemed to me that it would be better to let him see, to begin with, that I was not exactly poor, nor such an ungrateful cub as may be he had thought I was. It was my resolve that before we talked of anything else I would get that money off my conscience. I knew that then I could hold up my head, and discuss our neighborhood and old times, and it would be plain sailing for me. I had pictured to my mind a dozen times how uncle Jason would look with that new yellow buckskin bag crammed with gold on his knee, steadying it with his hand and talking to me. So when I got him up to my room, and seated him in a chair, I began the performance. I got red in the face, and spluttered, and flourished round with the bag and the gold; and, to tell the truth, I fully expected to make the old man's hair rise right up. But it did not work. He got shaky and trembled, and somehow did not seem to want the money at all, and finally owned how it was. He said that he had never given me a cent; it was all Lucy Cary's doing. And she had made him promise, on his everlasting Bible oath, as he called it, that he would not tell. She had put him up to the whole thing; even that first two-dollar bill had come from her wages."

My old classmate ceased speaking. He was becoming flushed and excited. He gazed abstractedly at the broad blue mirror of old Champlain, upon which he and I had looked together so often in the days of our youth.

Mr. Pember sat silently. Mrs. Pember was whimpering behind her handkerchief.

I ventured the inquiry, "Have you seen Lucy yet?"

Tompkins' face quivered; he was silent.

Mrs. Pember's interest in the question restored her. "Tell us, have you seen her?" she asked.

"I heard of it yesterday," Tompkins replied huskily, with an effort.

"Why, Timothy, what is the matter?" cried Mrs. Pember, rising from her seat and coming to him, as he bent his head and buried his face in his hands. The motherly woman took off his soft hat, and stroking his hair said, "You had better tell; it will do you good." And then she put his hat on again, and stood wiping her eyes in sympathy, while he struggled with himself.

The storm of feeling passed away, and Tompkins, having gained control of his emotions, slowly lifted his face from his hands, and sat peering out under his hat brim, looking apparently at a boat upon the lake. At last he said in a calm voice, "She is dead."

It was very still after this announcement. The softest breath of June scarcely whispered in the pines overhead, and the vast landscape below seemed strangely at rest in the fervid brightness of the summer noon.

My old classmate was the first to break the silence.

"Well," said he wearily, "it must be about time for dinner; let us go to the hotel."

We took the little brown road, and walked down a long, shaded, quiet street. Memories of college days and romantic summer nights, with music and starlight, and the long, long thoughts of youth came back to me, as I looked at the houses and gardens familiar in college days, and chatted about them with Mrs. Pember.

"Timothy always means well," said she to me confidentially, reverting to the subject of which we were all thinking, "but it was very wrong for him to neglect that poor factory girl; don't you think so?"

Mr. Toby's Wedding Journey

Mr. John Toby was a strong, hearty man,—I think a lumberman and ship-builder. I made his acquaintance in the course of a winter that I spent in Augusta, Maine.

His next appearance to me was in Hudson, a city of ten thousand people, situated on the east bank of the river, thirty miles below Albany. I was attending court in Hudson, and had my boy clerk, Cookie, with me. There came a rest because the cases were not ready, and we went away for a walk upon a public square or promenade. It was upon a bluff, which has a perpendicular face rising seventy feet above the river. Cookie and I seated ourselves upon a long bench placed there for the convenience of visitors, and gazed at the wide prospect.

In the foreground, at our feet, were the river and the boats, and on the farther shore the little village of Athens. Still beyond, a dozen miles away, we saw a wide, green, undulating valley, shut in by the bold, wooded Catskills. We saw the Mountain House,—like a white sheep dotting a green hill-side,—and knew that just below it is found the place where Rip Van Winkle slept so long. As we were speculating upon the exact place which Irving intended, Mr. Toby came climbing up a side path from the landing to where we were. Cookie and I were alone upon the promenade. Mr. Toby knew me at once, and I remembered his kind, genial face and keen, gray eye, and after a little I placed him correctly, and we shook hands very cordially.

"Glorious view,—is n't it?" he exclaimed with enthusiasm, turning toward the wide landscape.

We sat down and drifted into conversation.

After some general remarks Mr. Toby said,—

"I never was here but once before, and that was twelve years ago. I had the queerest time then I ever had in my life, and it comes back to me in the strangest way! Seeing this scenery is the reason, I suppose."

I encouraged him as adroitly as I could to tell us what he had on his mind.

"The truth is," he said, "I was on my wedding journey at that time. I may as well tell you about it. We came up the Hudson from New York on the day-boat, and of all delightful rides that is the best. It was in the middle of summer, just as it is now. They had music on board,—harps and fiddles; and it seemed to me the most entrancing combination of sounds I ever listened to. I suppose it *is* good on the water. There is a glory about a hot summer day here, as you ride along, and see the cities and mountains go by, that I never saw anywhere else. I imagine it must be like traveling in the Holy Land, or riding in a barge on the Nile in the time of Cleopatra.

"We left the boat here at Hudson, and came up on this promenade, and sat on this very bench. Sarah, because of being a little near-sighted, put on her glasses for a long shot, and was greatly taken with the view. She thought the mountains over there were the most interesting and beautiful sight she ever beheld. When we found in the guidebook that right down there below the Mountain House was where Rip Van Winkle slept, it seemed to us like fairy-land. I do not think it is possible to convey any idea of how happy we were. We had read of these things times enough, but to actually see them was more of a show than you might suppose.

"But there was one thing in the mean time that seemed strange. Right down *there,* near those iron-furnaces, by the landing, I got a glimpse of a fellow I had seen on the boat. I had not noticed him on the steamer particularly, but I remembered his looks when I saw him by that old building. He had a way of dodging behind something, whenever I turned my face toward him, that I had noticed on the boat, and I saw he did the same here, although he was so far away. My attention was called to him by that.

"After a while Sarah and I went down toward the landing to take the ferry and go over the river. We crossed, and one of the first things I saw after we got to Athens was that same young man, dodging behind a building. He must have sneaked across in some way without my seeing him. I thought that Sarah did not notice him, and I did not trouble her about it.

Mr. Toby's Wedding Journey

"We took a team, and had the most delightful wagon ride I ever had in my life, to Catskill village, and over toward the mountains. Sarah's aunty, Mrs. Robinson, a widow woman, was living in a little house near the foot of the mountain, and there was where we were going to put up. We had made arrangements to spend a month there. It is just impossible, I say again, to give you any idea of what a fairy-land it seemed to me. Sarah and I had both read up on this wonderful country just before we came. We almost expected to see Rip Van Winkle in the place they show, where he slept, about half-way up the mountain. Aunty Robinson was one of the kindest souls that ever lived. She took care of us as if we had been her own children. She got a team and a driver and took us to the Mountain House, and we went and saw the Falls and all the wonders. There were city people on the mountain and through the country everywhere, as there always are, I understand, up here at this time of year. It is handy by New York, you know, and a good place to run to in hot weather.

"Well, in the midst of all this, I saw, every now and then, that young man dodging out of sight. I would not have thought so much of it had it not been for one circumstance that gave point to it. The circumstance was this. One evening I went out of aunty's house to walk up the road a little ways alone, by moonlight. The mountains and the spruce-trees seem strangely like a panorama or a show-picture, when seen in that way. As I stepped out of the house and off the piazza, I saw that young man in the door-yard, speering around, and looking in at the windows. There was lamp-light inside, and he could see the folks. As I went across the yard to the front gate he turned and climbed the low fence and went off up the road. I confess that this worried me a little. I do not believe that any man who has been married less than a month can help thinking that his wife is a little more than common, and that the people are all anxious to get a look at her. I know my impression was that Sarah was better than other folks, and I never left her without feeling that it would be safer to lock her up so that nobody could carry her off. It seemed ridiculous to be jealous of that young man, and yet the question would come up, What he could be watching us for? I did not like it. If he was just a summer visitor, he ought to have manners. I determined to speak to him if he came around again looking into our windows. I do not think any ordinary affair would have made me bother aunty and Sarah with my troubles, but I *did* speak of this matter as soon as I got back to the house. I told them that a young man had been looking in the windows, and had run away when I saw him. Aunty thought it was nothing uncommon in the summer time, when so many visitors were in the neighborhood. But when I told her he had been in the door-yard she looked at it differently. She had missed a few things around the house, including some clothes spread on the grass to dry, and her suspicions were aroused.

"The next evening, and the next, I got a glimpse of

the young man again, hanging about the premises after dark. As he started off up the road in his customary manner, the third evening, I made bold to call out to him, 'Hullo there!' The moon was getting up a little later then, so that I had only a very dim sight of him. I could see, however, that he walked on without paying any attention, and disappeared in the shadow of the woods. I went into the house and related the incident. We felt that the thing was getting serious. It seemed clear that something ought to be done. We tried to get a little fun out of it by comparing the mysterious stranger to Rip Van Winkle, but Aunty said it was no joking matter. She insisted that this appearance was connected with the pilfering which had been going on for several weeks. When I presented the idea that the young man had probably come to the neighborhood only a few days before, as I had seen him on the boat near New York, she was not convinced.

"It was decided that the mystery ought to be fathomed in some way. We thought of telling the neighbors and stirring up public sentiment and organizing a watch, to catch the young man; but Aunty said she would not have the thing get out for the world. She thought it would be as bad as if the house were haunted. There was a multitude of idle people on the mountains and in the valley, who had come from the city for recreation, and they would catch up anything for a sensation. The idea of a house haunted by a mysterious young man would be as good as a ghost, and there would be an account of it in the newspapers within twenty-four hours if we made it known in the neighborhood. Aunty was really alarmed by the thought that the house might gain an unpleasant notoriety. Sarah and I promised that, whatever might happen, we would keep still about the young man. We all agreed in the opinion that the matter should be investigated. The plan was for me to stay out on the piazza in the shadow and watch, and Aunty, with her hired girl and Sarah, to be in the house in the usual way. If the mysterious stranger came into the yard, I was to speak to him, and if he started away, it would be my duty to follow him and get some sort of explanation. Sarah suggested that it was not safe for me to follow an unknown man off alone in the dark, and indeed it was not, but I was willing to risk it. The young fellow did not seem to me dangerous. He had a rather boyish face. It did come into my mind that a revolver would be handy, but I never carried one, and concluded to get along without it in this instance.

"It was quite dark when I took my place on the piazza under the shadow of some vines. Just at my right hand the window was partly open, and the light was streaming out. I had not been there ten minutes before the fellow put in an appearance. He came to the yard fence, and climbed over slowly. Then he advanced toward the piazza, and stood looking with the light from the window full in his face. He had a good enough countenance. It was plump and hard, without any great expression, and his mouth was straight and hard drawn.

He had short, dark hair. I would say he was not much used to being in the weather. He had no beard on his face, and seemed in other ways boyish. He wore a rough suit of dark woolen, and had a small, white, soft hat on his head.

"'Well, my friend,' said I, after a few moments, 'what can we do for you?'

"He was startled by the sound of my voice, and, turning away, went to the fence, put his hands on it, and climbed slowly over. Then he walked up the road toward the mountain. The three women inside, hearing my voice, came to the door. They were just in time to see me start in pursuit. I had provided myself with a very stout cane, which was in fact a club. Going out through the front gate into the darkness, I could see the young man, not more than two rods from me. It was pokerish, pursuing an individual who might turn at any moment and shoot me; but having undertaken the pursuit, it would not do for a newly married man to hesitate. The stranger quickened his pace until he began to run, and I followed him, keeping about a rod behind and talking to him. I asked him what he meant by haunting our premises night after night, and told him if he would stop and give an account of himself, that was all I wanted. I did not talk loud, but in a persuasive way, feeling a little scary, I confess. He ran for a quarter of a mile,—until we came to where there was woods on both sides of the road. Then he slowed up, kind of breathing hard, and I stepped a little nearer to him. By and by he stopped right in the road. It was not my plan to go close up, but I went within six or eight feet, keeping a good clinch hold of my club.

"'Who are you?' said I. 'What are you hanging around houses for in this way?'

"He answered in a light voice, 'You had better let me alone.'

"The moment he spoke, all the fear I had of him left me. To tell it just as it was, I began to scold him. It would do no harm if Aunty Robinson heard me. He did n't answer a word, but just stood and took it. Finally I told him, as I became eloquent, that it was a cowardly thing to sneak around and look into windows in the night, that he ought to be ashamed of himself; and that I would have him arrested. That seemed to rouse him, and he said again in that light voice of his, 'You had better let me alone.' I used a few more rough words, and he put his hand into the breastpocket of his coat. I thought he was after a pistol, and partly turned to run. But it was not that. He took out a large, yellow letter envelope, and handed it to me, saying, 'You may as well have it first as last. You can see me here tomorrow night if you come.'

"I was quite near to him, and took the envelope from his hand. The next moment he went into the woods, and I heard the brush crack as he poked away in the darkness, until the sound died in the distance, and he was gone.

"With the envelope in my hand, I went back to the

house, pluming myself on my boldness in the adventure, but feeling puzzled in regard to its termination. As I came to the gate the women were there waiting, and I remember to this day how Sarah welcomed me with a sly caress in the dark. I knew she was proud of me, and glad to have her aunty see that I was such a tremendous fellow. In the still summer night they had heard me talking loud up the road. I told them all about my hostile expedition, so to speak, and about the envelope, and we went into the house. We gathered around the table on which the lamp was standing, and examined the outside of the little package. There was no writing on it. It was not sealed, and Aunty pulled out the contents. Some old letters, apparently much worn by carrying, and a fresh piece of paper with a little writing on it, and a tintype came to the light.

"Now it is of no manner of use for me to tell you about women and how they act under trying circumstances. I will merely say that when Sarah saw the letters and the tin-type, and glanced at the writing on the fresh piece of paper, she gave a screech and everything was turned into confusion. Aunty Robinson began crying and yanking Sarah around, and they did everything that women could do to make a disturbance. The hired girl flew here and there in a fright. I tried to pull things into shape, but I could not seem to do the least thing, any more than if they had never seen me in their natural lives. Sarah did n't seem to even know who I was. It was half an hour before I could begin to get the thing through my head at all. And this was what the row was about. When I married Sarah she was, in a certain way, a kind of a widow. She came to Augusta, where I courted her, and told everybody about it. There was no concealment. I knew it perfectly well. There had been a boy in Portland, where she was brought up, named Amos Smith. He and Sarah had an engagement, boy and girl fashion. Along toward the last of the war, Amos got fired up with patriotism and a big bounty, and fear of the draft, and went to fight the battles of his country. But before he went, Sarah said she was not going to stay behind and risk being one of the girls who had to dangle along in the hope of a soldier by and by. She had seen too much of that sort of thing. It was now or never. And so, two hours before Amos started with his company for the South, he and some of the boys went over to Smith's, and the knot was tied good and strong.

"I may as well say here that I never had seen Amos Smith. But I am told that he was very pious, and everybody liked him. Young as he was, he used to lead the conference meetings sometimes. Perhaps they have made him out handsomer and better than he was. It is human nature to think well of the departed.

"As near as I can find out there was some crying and one thing and another, between Amos and Sarah when he left; but after the news came that he was among the crowd of killed and buried in the battles of the Wilderness, they tell me that she acted like a very sensible girl. She mourned of course, but she was proud of her noble boy, and his glorious death.

"And now you see the point. I married Sarah, or supposed I did, more than four years after Amos left this mortal sphere. And here he was coming to life again, by lamp-light, there in Aunty Robinson's house at the foot of the mountain, and those women were in a more distracted state than any other human beings I ever saw. Aunty Robinson had always lived in Portland, until two years before, so that she took in the whole thing at a glance.

"She finally explained it to me. That is, she did what she could toward it, between what you might call fainting spells, and sniffing at the camphor-bottle. I gave up trying to get anything out of Sarah, quite early in the investigation. She and Aunty had managed to put the papers and the tin-type out of sight, and they seemed entirely unable to comprehend my desire to examine them. Of course I ought to have looked at them first, but I was newly married, and did not understand that then. I had to take their word for it that Amos was still in the flesh. With a view to seeing the proofs, I took the liberty of doubting the fact; but I was showered with reproaches by aunty, and Sarah became more and more cold and forbidding. I had supposed, up to that time, that a married man, or one who had supposed he was married, still had the right to exercise private judgement, but I found out my mistake. It became clear to me that if I was intending to do anything with these women, I must *believe* that which they passionately asserted in regard to the bodily existence of Amos Smith. It was long after midnight before we got down to anything like rational talk. They did show me one thing at last. Aunty had received, that very afternoon, from Portland, a letter signed by an old neighbor, Jared Babcock, which conveyed a mysterious warning, that a strange thing had happened, and that we must be prepared for it. I will not deny that this letter knocked me completely over. We had a rough night of it, as you may guess. Aunty said, as it drew toward morning, that it seemed to her there could be only one right way. She looked wistfully at me as she said it. 'In the mean time,' she suggested, as if her meaning had been clear, 'Mr. Toby will not consider himself Sarah's husband.'

"Sarah was as pale as a white apron, and looked down and never said a word.

"It is not my way," explained Mr. Toby, taking his handkerchief from his pocket, "to make fun of serious subjects. If anybody wishes to know how I felt just then, all I can say is that I felt the very worst way,—the very worst."

I noticed that a tear stole down the cheek of the talker as he said this, and Cookie's bright, sympathetic face was very sorrowful.

"I had begun to understand," continued Mr. Toby, "that it was hard to be a bachelor before I married. I was thirty-four years old. I had never known what it was to really live until the last few months. It had been a great deal more to me than I can explain, to get away from a life of loneliness into the social sunshine. I had tried as a single man to carry my head high, but after I was thirty, the joke was always against me. And then there are sacred feelings which I will not mention. It seemed a bitter, cruel thing, to have all this end in a farce.

"But I was not wholly selfish. I do not mean to show myself worse than I was. I could not look at Sarah and think how she stood in the affair without a shudder. People would pity and they would laugh.

"As it began to be daylight, we pretended to go to rest. Aunty Robinson showed me into a little back bedroom, and took 'Mrs. Smith' with her, to her own room.

"This was felt to be right, but it was very trying to my feelings. It was *my* notion, first, to call Sarah Mrs. Smith. Perhaps there was a spice of malice in it. I do not think any man could keep his temper under the circumstances I have described. Of course I was sorry immediately after I had said Mrs. Smith. Yet it was received as all right and proper, which hurt me a great deal more than I would have been hurt by tears or reproaches.

"About ten o'clock in the morning we were moving about the house again. I do not think any one of us had touched a bed, but we made believe. We said, 'Good morning,' very ceremoniously. That is, Mrs. Robinson and I did. Sarah did not appear. Mrs. Robinson said, speaking in a formal manner, that Mrs. Smith was not feeling very well,—as if that was news! It soon appeared that Mrs. Robinson had reached a consoling conclusion, at which I also had arrived in my nightly reflections. She said, as we sat down to breakfast, that Amos must be induced to give up Sarah, if possible. The ceremony by which he had united himself to her had been merely a form, while Sarah and I were like old married folks, and it would not do in families of such high standing as ours, to break up the union. It must not be, on Sarah's account, if for no other reason. The good, kind soul urged and argued this point, just as if I were not already convinced, and more eager to accept the doctrine than she could be to have me.

"'I know Amos well,'" said Aunty. "'He is generous, and true-hearted, and poor. And he always was *so* conscientious! I hope it will not kill him to give up Sarah. I have already telegraphed to Sarah's father to come, and if he had not started for home, but was still in New York, he will be here to-morrow, you can be sure. The thing for you to do is to see Amos this evening, and talk the matter up. He has some claim. He let Sarah's brother have part of his bounty money, two hundred dollars, when he went away; and of course he ought to have it again, and *you* must be liberal.'

"'Dear Aunty Robinson,' said I with tears in my eyes, 'do you suppose money is of any account in such a matter as this?'

"She put down her knife and fork, looked at me through her glasses for a few seconds, and began to cry.

"The breakfast did not help us much. As to dinner, I do not think we had any; and how it ever came to be evening I cannot tell. But undoubtedly the sun went down as usual; for I remember that, after the longest day I ever spent in my life, it began to grow dark, and I started out toward the woods to meet Amos. There was one little circumstance occurred, just as I was starting, that married men will understand the force of. Sarah came out on the piazza in the dark, and took hold of me. I had not seen her at all during the day. When she slid from the door unexpectedly, and got me around the neck, it produced an effect on my feelings and nervous system that I will not try to describe. It makes me cry if I think of it too long, even now. It is enough to say, without going into particulars, that it became clear to me from that moment that I was still a married man, and I felt that Amos had no chance. I will merely mention, leaving out the details, that when Sarah left me, I found my club and started up the road, ready to smash Amos to flinders.

"I reached the appointed place in the edge of the woods, and waited a quarter of an hour in the dark and stillness. In the mean time my surplus courage ebbed away, and the real facts came before me. Just as I was reflecting upon the need of caution, I heard the brush crack in the woods, and a minute later I descried a form in the road.

"'Is that you?' I asked.

"'I am here,' replied Amos, in the same light voice, which I now remembered so well.

"We got into conversation immediately, and I said, 'You are Amos Smith, of Portland,' and he said, 'Yes, Mr. Toby, I am.' One thing led to another, until at last I asked him whether he could give up Sarah, or what his ideas were. He seemed to be a *still* kind of fellow, and did not answer me directly. It appeared as if he was willing to let me do all the talking. Finally, he asked if I would go with him into the woods, to his caboose as he termed it, where he said we could talk it over. I did not really like the idea, but I poked through the brush after him. He took me nearly half a mile to a kind of camp, where he had fixed a warm-weather sleeping place. There was a little fire burning on the ground, and some old boards leaning against a log, making a shelter under which he could crawl. He explained that he was hard up, and obliged to camp. We kind of lay down on the ground by the fire to talk. It was as strange a place as I ever was in. The queer thing about Amos was his extreme reticence. I had to introduce every subject. Finally, I asked him square whether there was not some way we could arrange it about Sarah, provided property matters could be made all right in his favor. Then, for the first time, Amos made a speech. He said he knew it was a dreadful thing for him to come down on me the way he had, but that he had been compelled to do it. Sickness and other terrible calamities of some indefinite sort were alluded to. It was on my tongue to ask him where he had been all this time, and how it happened that he was not killed, and why they had not heard from him in Portland; but before I had time to do that, he concluded his speech in the following remarkable words, which knocked everything else out of my mind:—

"'And now, Mr. John Toby, of Augusta, Maine, I am not a man who trifles. If you bring me seven hundred dollars within three days, you will never see me again. I will go West, and send you a copy of the divorce papers, so that you can marry your wife legally and all right. But if you don't, I shall go and see her; and if she and I, or her folks and I, meet, that is the end of it. I shall claim her and have my rights. You can take your choice. There it is, and I mean just what I say. If you have any change with you to bind the bargain, that will be our contract.'

"I do not claim to be unusually bright," said Mr. Toby, looking keenly at me and then at Cookie; "but when I heard that speech I comprehended. The words and manner, and everything about it, seemed like a dime-novel. It was anything but natural. And I claim that the fact that I was sitting by a miserable, lying, thieving vagabond was made just as plain to me that minute, as though I had known him a thousand years. The whole thing flashed upon me, as if I had been struck by lightning. The folks will try to have it to this day, that I did n't understand it at the time; but I did, although I had presence of mind enough to restrain my feelings. If the other fellow had been reticent, it was my turn now, and I sat as glum and still as a stump, and looked at the fire. Of course I don't deny that I agreed with him that I would see about raising the seven hundred dollars, and I was justified in doing that. But what I claim is, that after he made that speech the whole thing seemed to me like the side-show to a circus. I did not believe in it.

"It would be nonsense for me to deny," continued

Mr. Toby, reddening, "that I gave him what loose change I had in my pocket. But then he was in destitution, and I would have given him that anyway. It is true I had left my pocket-book at the house, but the idea that I would have given that scamp any great amount of money is preposterous. We arranged that I could come at any time and see him at his caboose, and pay him the money. He said he would be there most of the time, and if he was away I could wait for him. I was to meet him every evening at any rate, in the road. He showed me the way for a few rods, and then we parted, and I went back, all right, to the house.

"Now I knew perfectly well that it would be useless to try to convince those women that the chap I had talked with was not the sainted Amos, and I had no proof but what he was. I did not know of any way to make it plain to them that he was a vagabond and a fraud. And so I let it go that he *was* Amos, and told them it was all right, and that he only wanted seven hundred dollars. Aunty was dissolved in tears at the moderation of the conscientious young man, and hoped I had not been too hard with him. Sarah wiped her eyes with her apron, and said she was sure her father would pay it, because he and her brother had part of Amos's bounty money. When I explained that Amos was camping in the woods because he was without means, Mrs. Robinson was so affected by the noble character suggested, that she not only shed tears, but went to her pantry and lighted her globe lantern, insisting that I should take it and go back through the woods and pilot the poor boy to the hotel, which was a mile away. It was all I could do to persuade her out of it.

"There is no use of spinning out a story," said Mr. Toby, rising and gazing up the river, with the avowed object of seeing whether the down boat for New York was coming. As the boat was not in sight, he sat down again, and resumed as follows:—

"Well, we slept some that night, and the next day waited for Sarah's father to come, before doing anything. He came in the afternoon. He was a cool-headed man, and had seen a thing or two. He heard all the women had to say, and compelled them to let him see all they had to show in the way of evidence. Then he and I went out in the wood shed. He looked me straight in the eye, and, said he, 'John, do you think that fellow is Amos Smith?' I said, 'No, I don't.' And he said, 'Nor I either.' And he said, 'Amos was killed in the war. And how it happens that this fellow has got hold of Sarah's letters I don't know, but I dare say he was acquainted with Amos in the army. It is queer all round. I think some of the writing is a forgery. I don't believe Jared Babcock ever wrote that letter; and that new letter cannot have been written by Amos, although it is like his writing, I must say.'"

The narrator paused a moment, as if reflecting.

"Did you find out who it was afterward?" asked Cookie eagerly.

"Wait until you hear," said Mr. Toby. "The short of

it is, I was sent at evening to meet Amos, or whoever he was, again. But he failed to come that time. So the next morning I went up to his caboose before breakfast, bound to find out the facts. I had more than a hundred different things enjoined upon me to do and to ask before I started. Between Aunty and Sarah's father, there was no end to the instructions. They were laying all kinds of traps to find out whether it was Amos.

"Well, I got to the place all right, and looked around. It did not seem so pokerish by daylight. There was no fire burning, and I could see that it had been out a good while, for there was no smoke.

"We had been planning, before I left the house, to have the whole party creep up sometime during the day behind the bushes, and see if it was Amos, while I talked with him. So I looked around to find out if there was a place handy where they could hide. Then I stepped up to where the boards were, and stooped down and looked under them. I saw something there, and stooping lower, it became clear that it was a man, and then, that it was the one I was looking for. He did not move when I spoke. I thought at first he was asleep, and imagined I heard a snore."

"Was he drunk?" asked Cookie.

"I am not going to work up an excitement over this thing," continued Mr. Toby, with a serious air. "To be plain about it, he was just lying there, a stark, cold, dead man. Of course it gave me an awful kind of shock to find him there alone. But I had found a boy that way once before, off in a lot up in Maine; and I don't think I was as much worked up over it this time as most folks would have been. I had seen a good deal of that kind of thing too, in a hospital, at one time.

"We gave notice, and there was an inquest according to law. And it was found out that the fellow was just the kind of a vagabond I had thought he was. Whether he died of heart disease, or by taking some of the drugs found in his vest pocket, was not exactly clear. It was told by somebody, and found to be true, that he had served a three years' term at Sing Sing, just down the river here, and had only been out of prison two months."

Mr. Toby ceased his narrative, and looked contemplatively toward the mountains, apparently absorbed in thought. I was about to speak when he said,—

"I have told you this just as it seemed at the time. But there was a secret in it that we kept close for a long while, and nobody suspected. Before we gave notice, Sarah's father and Aunty and Sarah and I went to get a look at the dead man. They wanted to see who it was. We crept slyly through the woods. It was a bright sunshiny morning. As we came near the place, there was a dry, mossy spot where Aunty and Sarah sat down to wait, while Sarah's father and I went ahead to see. When we got to the caboose I pulled a board away, and let in the bright light. Sarah's father put on his specs and got down pretty close to look. When he straightened up, I could see that something was the matter. And as true as I sit here, and after all I have told you, that poor, miserable, prison-bird and vagabond was Amos Smith, of Portland, Maine,—and may God have mercy on his soul!"

Mr. Toby evidently felt this announcement to be a very important one. His voice was broken as he uttered it; his large hands trembled, and soon his feelings found relief in tears.

We sat for a while longer, and heard how Amos had been put away in a corner of a little yard, where his folks could find him if they should ever care to, and how his history had been concealed from them until the sharpest sting of it had passed away. All the public ever knew of it was that a tramp from Sing Sing had been found dead near the road. It was not an unusual occurrence in this thronged and busy valley. A careless newspaper paragraph was the sole record of the event.

"Did n't want to live, did he?" suggested Cookie, in a pause of the conversation.

"That is just what I tell the folks," responded Mr. Toby. "When he saw Sarah, I suppose it brought back old times. I do not wonder that he crept around and peeked in through the window. It is my opinion that he ended his days with the drugs; I have no doubt of it. And it makes my heart ache when I think of the boy dying alone over there in the woods,—Hullo, there comes the down boat, and I must go. I am traveling alone this time, and just walked up here to wait. This talk has done me a world of good. If you ever come our way, call. Good-by, sir, good-by." And with a shake of the hand for each of us, he was gone.

We watched him as he hastened down the path to the landing, and as he went on board; then we watched the steamer as it bore him southward, while he stood on deck waving his yellow handkerchief and bowing farewell. The soft notes of a flute and the music of harps and of viols came back to us from the boat, as it was slipping away through the blue gleaming water.

As we looked and listened the form of Mr. Toby blended with the crowd, and the dulcet sounds fainted and died in the sunshine. Then Cookie and I discussed our visitor's story. Except the wedding feature, how like it was to the dull monotony of a narrative that is constantly repeated in the cities of the valley:

A poor boy from a far country came to this fairyland; he dreamed, he forgot the light of home, he wandered and is lost.

In Slavery Days

First, as my grandfather used to tell, there were the woods and the Oneida Indians and the Mohawks; then the forest was cleared away, and there was the broad, fertile, grassy, and entrancingly beautiful Mohawk Valley; then came villages and cities and my own unimportant existence, and at about the same time appeared the Oneida Institute. This institution of learning is my first point. The Oneida Institute, located in the village of Whitesboro, four miles from Utica, in the State of New York, consisted visibly of three elongated erections of painted, white-pine clapboards, with shingle roofs. Each structure was three stories high and was dotted with lines of little windows. There was a surrounding farm and gardens, in which the students labored, that might attract attention at certain hours of the day, when the laborers were at work in them; but the buildings were the noticeable feature. Seated in the deep green of the vast meadows on the west bank of the willow-shaded Mohawk, these staring white edifices were very conspicuous. The middle one was turned crosswise, as if to keep the other two, which were parallel, as far apart as possible. This middle one was also crowned with a fancy cupola, whereby the general appearance of the group was just saved to a casual stranger from the certainty of its being the penitentiary or almshouse of the country.

The glory of this institution was not in its architecture or lands, but in that part which could not be seen by the bodily eyes. For, spiritually speaking, Oneida Institute was an immense battering-ram, behind which Gerrit Smith, William Lloyd Garrison, and Rev. Beriah Green were constantly at work, pounding away to destroy the walls which slavery had built up to protect itself.

Mr. Green was president of the institute, and was the soul and heart and voice of the faculty. His power to mould young men was phenomenal. It was a common saying that he turned out graduates who were the perfect echo of Beriah Green, except the wart. The wart was a large one, which, being situated in the centre of Mr. Green's forehead, seemed to be a part of his method to those who were magnetized by his personality or persuaded by his eloquence.

Perhaps about two students in each hundred at the Institute would be colored.

About 1845, when I began to be an observing boy, it was understood throughout Oneida County that Beriah Green was an intellectual giant, and that he would sell his life, if need be, to befriend the colored man. Oneida Institute was a refuge for the oppressed, quite as much as a place where the students were magnetized and taught to weed onions. Fifteen years before John Brown paused in his march to the gallows to kiss a negro baby, I saw Beriah Green walk hand in hand along the sidewalk with a black man and fondle the hand he held conspicuously. Among his intimates were Ward and Garnet, both very black, as well as very talented and very eloquent.

We were taught that it was a matter of duty to subdue our feelings of prejudice against color. Young as I was I am sure I came to sympathize truly with the black man, and with those who advocated the abolition of slavery.

When "the friends of the cause" met in convention, I sometimes heard of it, and managed, boy-like, to steal in. When I did so, I used to sit and shudder on a back seat in the little hall. The anti-slavery denunciations poured out upon the churches, and backed up and pushed home by the logic of Green and the eloquence of Smith, were well calculated to make an orthodox boy tremble. For these people brought the churches and the nation before their bar and condemned them, and some whom I have not named cursed them with a bitterness and effectiveness that I cannot recall to this day without a shiver. The dramatic effect, as it then seemed to me, has never been equaled in my experience.

That these extreme ideas did not prosper financially is not to be wondered at. The farm was soon given up, then the buildings and gardens passed into other hands, and the institution became a denominational school,

In Slavery Days 177

known as the Whitestown Baptist Seminary. But the ideas which had been implanted there would not consent to depart with this change in the name and the methods of the institution. The fact that Beriah Green, after leaving the school, continued to reside at Whitesboro and gathered a church there rendered it the more difficult to eradicate the doctrines which he had implanted. The idea of friendship for the black man was particularly tenacious and perhaps annoying to the new and controlling denominational interest. It clung to the very soil, like "pusley" in a garden. It had gained a strong hold throughout the county. The managers of the institution could not openly oppose it. They were compelled to endure it. And so it continued to be true that if a bright colored boy anywhere in the state desired the advantages of a superior education he would direct his steps to Whitestown Seminary.

It was here that I met the hero of my story, Anthony Calvert Brown. He was as vigorous and manly a youth of seventeen as I have ever seen. He had been among us nearly two months, and had become a general favorite, before it was discovered that he had a tinge of African blood. The revelation of this fact was made to us on the playground. A fellow-student who had come with Anthony to the school made the disclosure. The two were comrades, and had often told us of their adventures together in the great North woods, or Adirondack forests, on the western border of which, in a remote settlement, they had their homes. Their friendship did not prevent them from falling into a dispute, and it did not prevent Anthony's comrade, who was in fact a bully, from descending to personalities. He hinted in very expressive terms that the son of a colored woman must not be too positive. The meanness of such an insinuation, made at such a time and in such a way, did not diminish its sting. Perhaps it increased it. We saw Anthony, who had stood a moment before cool and defiant, turn away cowed and subdued, his handsome face painfully suffused. His behavior was a confession.

I am sorry to say that after this incident Anthony did not hold the same position in our esteem that he had previously enjoyed. Some half-dozen of us who cherished the old Institute feeling were inclined to make a hero of him, but by degrees the sentiment of the new management prevailed, and it was understood that Anthony was to be classed with those who must meekly endure an irreparable misfortune. But Anthony did not seem to yield to this view. He was very proud, and braced himself firmly against it. He withdrew more and more from his schoolmates and devoted his time to books. In the matter of scholarship he gained the highest place, and held it to the close of our two-years' course. In the meantime, his peculiarities were often made the subject of remark among us. His growing reserve and dignity, his reputation as a scholar, and his reticence and isolation were frequently discussed. And there was the mystery of his color. It was a disputed question among us whether the African taint could be detected in his appearance. Ray, the comrade who had revealed it, claimed that it was plainly perceptible, while Yerrinton, the oldest student among us, declared that there was not a trace of it to be seen. He argued that Anthony was several shades lighter than Daniel Webster, and he asserted enthusiastically that he had various traits in common with that great statesman. But, then, Yerrinton was a disciple of Beriah Green, and his opinion was not regarded as unbiased. For myself, I could never detect any appearance of African blood in Anthony, although my knowledge of its existence influenced my feelings toward him. To me he seemed to carry himself with a noble bearing,—under a shadow, it is true, yet as if he were a king among us. I remember thinking that his broad forehead, slightly Roman nose, mobile lips, and full features wore a singularly mournful and benevolent expression, like the faces sometimes seen in Egyptian sculpture.

I did not discuss the matter of his peculiarities with Anthony freely until after our school-days at the seminary were ended and he had left Whitestown. His first letter to me was a partial revelation of his thoughts upon the subject of his own character and feelings. He had gone to Philadelphia to teach in a large school, while I remained with my relatives in Whitesboro. He wrote me that he was troubled in regard to certain matters of which he had never spoken to any one, not even to me, and he thought it would be a good thing for him to present them for consideration, if I was willing to give him the benefit of my counsel. In reply I urged that he should confide in me fully, assuring him of my desire to assist him to the utmost of my ability.

The communication which I received in response to my invitation was to some extent a surprise. The letter was a very long one, and very vivid and expressive. He began it by alluding to the incident upon the playground, which had occurred nearly two years before. He said that his life had been guarded, up to about that time, from feeling the effects of the misfortunes which attach to the colored race. Living in a remote settlement and a very pleasant home, where all were free and equal and social distinctions almost unknown, he had scarcely thought of the fact that his mother was an octoroon. He had heard her talk a great deal about those distinguished French gentlemen who had in the early part of the century acquired lands in the vicinity of his home, and he had somehow a feeling that she had been remotely connected with them, and that his own lineage was honorable. He alluded specifically to Le Ray de Chaumont and Joseph Bonaparte. These two men, and others, their countrymen, who had resided or sojourned upon the edge of the great wilderness near his birthplace, had been his ideals from childhood. He had often visited Lake Bonaparte, and had frequently seen the home formerly occupied by Le Ray. While he had understood that he himself was only plain Anthony C. Brown, the son of Thomas Brown (a white man who had died some two months before his son's birth), he had yet an impression that his mother was in some vague way connected with the great personage whom he mentioned. How it was that Thomas Brown had come to marry his mother, or what the details of her early life had been, he did not know, being, in fact, ignorant of his family history. He conceded that it might be only his own imagination that had led him to suppose that he was in some indefinite way to be credited with the greatness of those wealthy land proprietors who had endeavored to establish manorial estates or seigniories in the wilderness. He had come to understand that this unexplainable impression of superiority and connection with the great, which had always been with him in childhood and early youth, was due to his mother's influence and teaching. There was about it nothing direct and specific, and yet it had been instilled into his mind, in indirect ways, until it was an integral part of his existence. His mother had a farm and cattle and money. She was in better circumstances than her neighbors. This had added to his feeling of superiority and independence. The accident of a slight tinge of color had hardly risen even to the dignity of a joke in the freedom of the settlement and the forest. Looking back, he believed that his mother had guarded his youthful mind against receiving any unfavorable impression upon the subject. In his remote, free, wilderness home he had heard but little of African slavery, and had regarded it as a far-off phantom, like heathendom or witchcraft.

Such had been the state of mind of Anthony Brown.

The light had, however, been gradually let in upon him in the course of an excursion which he and his comrade Ray had made the year previous to their appearance at Whitestown Seminary. In that excursion they had visited Chicago, Cleveland, Niagara Falls, Buffalo, Syracuse, Rochester, New York, and Albany. They had strayed into a court-room in the City Hall at Albany, where many people were listening to the argument of counsel who were discussing the provisions of the will of a wealthy lady, deceased. A colored man was mixed up in the matter in some way,—probably as executor and legatee. Anthony heard with breathless interest the legal disabilities of colored people set forth, and their inferior social position commented upon. He learned that the ancestral color descended to the children of a colored mother, although they might appear to be white. These statements had impressed him deeply. They furnished to his mind an explanation of the various evidences of the degradation of the colored people he had seen upon his journey. Talking of these matters, he had found that Ray was much better informed than himself upon the entire subject. Ray, in fact, frankly explained that a colored man had no chance in this country. This was in 1854. Anthony suggested in his letter to me that he had probably been kept from acquiring this knowledge earlier in life by his mother's anxious care and the kindness of friends and neighbors. He explained that he did not mean to be understood as intimating that he had not some general knowledge of the facts previously, but it was this experience which had made him feel that slavery was a reality and that all colored people belonged to a despised race. After his return home he had carefully refrained from imparting to his mother any hint of his newly-acquired impressions in reference to the social and legal standing of the colored race. In the enjoyment of home-comforts, and in the freedom of the wild woods and waters, the shadow which had threatened in his thoughts to descend upon him passed away. He remembered it only as a dream which might not trouble him again, and which he would not cherish. Still, there was a lurking uneasiness and anxiety, born of the inexorable facts, which favorable circumstances and youthful vivacity could not wholly overcome.

In this state of mind Anthony, in accordance with the wish of his mother, came to Whitestown Seminary. His description of his first impressions there was very glowing. He wrote:—

"I cannot hope, my dear friend, to give you any adequate idea of what I then experienced. For the first time in my life I found kindred spirits. Your companionship in particular threw a light upon my pathway that made the days all bright and gave me such joy as I had never before known. And there was Ralph, so kind and true, and Henry Rose, so honest and faithful! I cannot tell you how my heart embraced them. It is a simple truth, telling less than I felt, when I say that I could scarcely sleep for thinking of my new-found treasures. You need to remember what it is to dwell in a rough country, isolated and remote from towns, to appreciate my experience. To me, coming to Whitestown was a translation to Paradise. It seems extravagant, yet it is true, that I met there those who were dearer than my life and for whom I would have died. The first warm friendships of youth are the purest and whitest flowers that bloom in the soul. If these are blighted, it is forever. Such flowers in any one life can never grow again.

"And this brings me to that sad day when on the playground Ray struck at me, and through me at my dear, loving mother. As he spoke those cruel words, the world grew dark about me, the dread fear which I had subdued revived with tenfold power, and upon my heart came the pangs of an indescribable anguish. Oh, the chill, the death-like chill, that froze the current of my affections as I saw the faces of those I loved averted!

"I went to my room and tried to reflect, but I could not. The shock was too great. During the week that followed I was most of the time in my silent room. I may well call it silent, for the footsteps to which I had been accustomed came no more, and the comrades in whose friendship I had such delight no longer sought my company. That dreadful week was the turning-point in my life. As it drew toward its close I realized to some extent what I had been through, as one does who is recovering from a severe illness. I knew that day and night I had wept and moaned and could see no hope, no ray of light, and that I had at times forgotten my religion and blasphemed. It is true, my dear friend, that I mocked my God. Do not judge me hastily in this. I was without discipline or experience, and I saw that for all sorrow except mine there was a remedy. Even for sin there is repentance and redemption, and the pains of hell itself may be avoided. But for my trouble there could be no relief. The thought that I was accursed from the day of my birth, that no effort, no sacrifice, no act of heroism on my part could ever redeem me, haunted my soul, and I knew that it must haunt me from that time onward and forever.

"I need hardly tell you, with your insight and knowledge, that these inward struggles led toward a not unusual conclusion. I allude to the determination to which multitudes of souls have been driven in all ages to escape the tortures of disgrace. I turned away from humanity and sought that fearful desert of individual loneliness and isolation which is now more sad and real to me than any outward object can be. To live in the voiceless solitude and tread the barren sands unfriended is too much for a strong man with all the aids that philosophy can give him. But when we see one in the first flush of youth, wholly innocent, yet turning his footsteps to the great desert to get away from the scorn of lovers and friends, and when we realize that this which he dreads must continue to the last hour of his life, there is to my mind a ghastliness about it as if it were seen in the light of the pit which is bottomless. I have not recovered, and can never recover, from that experience. You will infer, however, that I did not remain in just the condition of mind which I have endeavored to describe. He whom I had blasphemed came to me, and I was penitent. The teachings of good Father Michael at our home, the doctrines of our Church, and the examples of the blessed saints, were my salvation. Then I felt that I would dwell alone with God. And there was something grand about that, and very noble. The purest joy of life is possible in such an experience. Yet it is not enough, especially in youth. But I think I should have continued in that frame of mind had it not been for you and Ralph. How you two came to me and besought my friendship I need not remind you. Neither need I say how my pride yielded; and if there was anything to forgive I forgave it, and felt the light of friendship, which had been withdrawn from my inner world, come back with a joy that has increased as it has continued.

"Coming to this city of 'brotherly love,' I begin my life anew, and at the very threshold a painful question meets me. No faces are averted, no one suspects my social standing. A thrill of kindness is in every voice. What can I do? Must I advertise myself as smitten with a plague? I dare not tell you of the favors that society bestows upon me. It is but little more than a month since I came to Philadelphia, and during that short period I have in some strange way become popular. My sincere effort politely to avoid society seems only to have resulted in precipitating a shower of invitations upon me. Evidently the fact that I am tinged with African blood is wholly unsuspected. You understand, I think, how I gained this place as teacher in the school. It was through the interposition of Father Michael and certain powerful Protestant friends of his who are unknown to me. It was not my own doing, and I do not feel that I am to blame. But I will frankly tell you that it seems to me cowardly to go forward under false colors. One thing I am resolved upon,—I will never be ashamed of my dear mother. Where I go she shall go, and she shall come here if she is inclined to do so. As you have never seen her, I may say that she is regarded as dark for an octoroon, and with her presence no explanation will be necessary. But ought I to wait for that? She may not choose to come. How can I best be an honest man? It seems silly, and it would be ridiculous, to give out generally here as a matter for the public that I am the son of a negro woman. Yet I think it must come to that in some way. What shall I do?"

This letter caused me to think of Anthony and his trouble much more seriously than before. It was clear to me why he was popular. I had never met any young man who was by nature more sympathetic and attractive. The reserve and sadness which had recently come upon him were not to his disadvantage socially. They rather tended to gain attention and win the kindness of strangers. The question which his position presented, and about which he desired my counsel, troubled me. But, fortunately, after thinking of it constantly for two days, I gave him advice which I still think correct under the circumstances. I argued that he was not under any obligation to advertise himself to the public as a colored man. The public did not expect or require this of any one. But I urged that if he made any special friends among those who entertained him socially and with whom he was intimate, he should frankly make known to them the facts in regard to his family. I thought this would be expected, and I was convinced that such a presentation of his position, made without affectation, would win for him respect even from those who might cease to court his society. I further urged that he ought not, as a teacher, to isolate himself or shun those relations with families which would place upon him the obligation to make known his parentage.

Anthony sent a brief note in reply to my letter, thanking me heartily for what he termed my convincing statement, and expressing his determination to act in accordance with it.

Nearly two months passed, and then my friend communicated the further fact that he had gone so far, in several instances, and with several families, as to carry out the suggestions I had made. He thought it was too soon to assert what the ultimate result would be, but stated the immediate effects so far as he could see them. When he first made the announcement in regard to his color, many had disbelieved it. When his persistent and repeated declarations upon various occasions had convinced his friends that it was not a jest, but a reality, they had been variously affected by it. He thought some were politely leaving him, while others seemed desirous of continuing his acquaintance.

Ten days later I was not a little surprised to receive a letter conveying the information that Anthony's mother had arrived in Philadelphia in response to his invitation. He stated, in his letter to me giving this news, that he had now carried out his entire plan and was satisfied. His mother had visited his school, and he had introduced her to his various friends in the city. It seemed to me a mistake thus unnecessarily to run the risk of offending social preferences or prejudices; but I did not feel at liberty to comment upon the matter at the time.

In addition to the information conveyed, the letter contained an invitation which delighted me. Anthony wrote that he and his mother were about returning home. The long vacation would begin in a few days, and they wished that I should go with them for a visit. Few things could have afforded me greater satisfaction than this. The wild forest-country, of which my schoolmate had told me much, I regarded as peculiarly a region of romance and adventure.

My aunt objected to this visit, on the ground that it would not be well for me to associate with people of an inferior race or doubtful color. But the great sinfulness of this prejudice (as explained by Gerrit Smith, Mr. Garrison, and Beriah Green) was so strongly urged, that she permitted me to make the journey.

It was a beautiful morning early in July when we

three, with a team and a driver, left the Mohawk Valley and climbed the Deerfield hills, making our way northward. On the evening of the first day we reached the hills of Steuben and gained a first glimpse of that broad, beautiful forest-level, known as the Black-River country, which stretches away toward the distant St. Lawrence. The next day we descended to this level, and following the narrow road through forests, clearings, and little settlements, and villages, arrived just at nightfall at the home of my friends. It was a small, unpainted, wooden house, standing near the road. Back of it were barns and sheds, and I saw cattle and sheep grazing. The zigzag rail fence common to the region surrounded the cleared lots in sight, and in front of the house, across the road, were the wild woods. A wood-thrush was pouring out his thrilling, liquid notes as we arrived. A white woman and a large, black shaggy dog came out of the house to welcome us; and a few minutes later I had the best room, upstairs over the front door, assigned to me, and was a guest in the domicile of my friend Anthony.

The location was a delightful one, about three miles west of the little village of Champion, near which was a small lake, where we spent many morning hours. From a height not far away we had glimpses, in clear weather, of the mountains, seen in airy outline toward the eastward.

My friend had the horses and wagons of the farm at his command, and we took many long rides to visit places of interest. On several occasions we saw the decaying château of Le Ray, which was but little more than an hour's ride to the northward of Anthony's home; and on one occasion we went a day's journey and saw the stony little village of Antwerp, and visited that beautiful sheet of water on the margin of the wilderness, known as Lake Bonaparte. Joseph Bonaparte frequently visited this lake, and he owned lands in its vicinity, and made some improvements upon them in 1828.

Anthony's mother was a tall, spare woman, with a wrinkled face and large, straight features. She seemed to me a curious mixture of European features with a dark skin. She used French phrases in a peculiar way, and was full of the history of Le Ray and Bonaparte and various members of the company that had undertaken to make of this section, in years gone by, a rich and fertile country like the Mohawk Valley. It appeared that the name which the company had given to this region was Castorland, which she interpreted to mean the land of the beaver. She had, among other curiosities, some coins or tokens which had been stamped in Paris on behalf of the company, and on which the "Castorland," accompanied by suitable devices was plainly seen. The one that interested me most seemed to have as its device the representation of a small dog trying to climb a tree. I was informed, however, that the animal was a beaver, and that he was cutting down the tree with his teeth.

After talking freely with the mother, Antoinette Brown, I did not wonder that Anthony had learned to honor the gentlemen who had come from France to this region in early days as among the greatest men in the world. I did not find myself able to discredit her realistic and vivid description of the visits of Joseph Bonaparte to his wilderness domain in a six-horse chariot, followed by numerous retainers. Neither did I find myself able to disbelieve in the accuracy of her picturesque description of Joseph Bonaparte's Venetian gondola floating upon the waters of Northern New York, or her account of his dinner-service of "golden plate" spread out by the roadside on one memorable occasion when he paused in his kingly ride and dined in a picturesque place near the highway. She told in a convincing manner many traditions relating to the enterprise which was to have made of the Black-River country a rich farming region not inferior to the Mohawk Flats. The fact that nature had not seconded this undertaking had not diminished Mrs. Brown's impressions of its magnitude and importance. The great tracts which had been purchased and the great men who had purchased them were vividly impressed upon her imagination. In reference to her personal history, except for a few allusions to life in New York City, she was reticent.

I remained nearly two months at the home of my friend, and became familiar with the places of interest surrounding it. The little lake was a memorable spot, for there Anthony first told me the full story of his experiences in Philadelphia. He did not conceal the fact that an attachment was growing up between himself and the daughter of his best friend there, Mr. Zebina Allen. The way to make his permanent home in the Quaker City seemed to be opening before him. That I should go with him for a few days to Philadelphia when he returned, to "see how the land lay," as he expressed it in backwoods phrase, was one of his favorite ideas. He made so much of this point that I finally consented to accompany him.

It was a rainy day early in September when we stepped off the cars and went to Anthony's boarding-place in the good old city that held the one he loved and his fortunes. I was introduced to various friends of his, and during the first twenty-four hours of my sojourn I was delighted with all matters that came under my observation. I was especially pleased with Mr. Allen and his daughter Caroline. But within two days I saw, or fancied that I saw, a curious scrutiny and reserve in the faces of some of those with whom we conversed.

I think Anthony was more surprised than I was when he received a note from one of the trustees intimating that important changes were likely to be made in reference to the educational methods to be employed in the school, and that, in view of these changes, it was barely possible that some new arrangements in regard to teachers might be desired by the patrons of the institution. The trustee professed to have written this information in order that "Mr. Brown" might not be taken wholly by surprise in case any step affecting his position should be found advisable.

The circumlocution and indefiniteness of this letter led me to infer that there was something behind it which the writer had not stated. It soon appeared that my friend agreed with me in this inference. I could not but smile at the coolness with which he quoted the common phrase to the effect that there was an African in the fence.

"I fear it is the old story over again," he said; "but I am glad I have done my duty to myself and to my dear mother, whatever the consequences may be."

After some discussion, it was agreed that I should call at Mr. Allen's office (he was a lawyer) and endeavor to obtain from him a statement of all he might know of the new arrangement announced in the letter which had been received. I lost no time in entering upon my mission. But I was compelled to make several applications at the office before it was possible for Mr. Allen to give me a hearing. A late hour of the business-day was, however, finally assigned to me, and just as the gas was lighted I found myself by appointment in a private room used for consultation, sitting face to face with Mr. Allen. I briefly stated my errand, and presented the trustee's letter to him as a more complete explanation of my verbal statement.

"Yes, I see," said Mr. Allen thoughtfully, after reading the letter and returning it to me. And he tilted back his chair, clasped his hands behind his head, and gazed for some minutes reflectively at the ceiling. I sat quietly and studies his face and the objects in the room. He was a large man, squarely built, with straight, strongly-marked features, blue eyes, and sandy hair. In the midst of his books and papers he seemed to me a sterner man than I had previously thought him. "Yes, I see," he repeated, at the close of his period of reflection. And then he removed his hands from his head and placed them on his knees, and brought his chair squarely to the floor, and, leaning forward toward me, looked keenly in my face, and said, "Did I understand that you were one of those people,—that is, similar to Mr. Brown?"

"How, sir?" said I in bewilderment. "How do you mean?"

A moment later the purport of the question dawned fully upon me, or I should rather say struck me, so sharp and sudden was the shock I experienced. If there was anything in which I was secure and of which I had reason to be proud, it was my Puritan and English ancestry. As the blood flew to my youthful face in instinctive protest and indignation, my appearance must have been a sufficient answer to my interrogator; for I remember that he, at once springing to his feet, offered me his hand, making profuse apologies and begging a thousand pardons.

I somewhat stammeringly explained that it was of no consequence, and proceeded to name the families in my ancestral line, adding the remark that these families, both those on my father's side and those on my mother's side, were pretty well known, and that they were the genuine English and Puritan stock.

"They are indeed, sir," said Mr. Allen, "and I congratulate you. I know the value of a good lineage, and I feel safe in talking freely with a gentleman of your standing in regard to this disagreeable business."

I found myself taking sides with Mr. Allen in favor of family pride and against "those people," as he had termed persons of doubtful color. I had instinctively defended myself against the suggestion that I might possibly be one of them. If this skillful lawyer had intended, as possibly he did, to disarm me wholly at the outset, so that I could make no attack upon the position which he intended to assume, he could not have done it more effectually.

"The truth is," said Mr. Allen cheerfully, "we regard Mr. Brown as about the best and most intelligent young man that has ever taught in our school. He is manly and conscientious to a fault. Aside from his family, the only trouble I find with him is that he is not politic. It was very honorable in him to state to us his parentage as he did. If he had been willing to stop there, possibly we might have managed it,—at least so far as the school was concerned. But it was not necessary and it was not wise to bring that colored woman here. It may have been remarkably filial and brave, and all that, but it was not judicious. I think you will agree with me that it was not judicious."

I hesitatingly admitted that it probably was not.

"I felt sure that you would take a sensible view of the matter," said Mr. Allen. "I am truly sorry that Mr. Brown could not have been more discreet. If he has imagined that he could push that woman into our society, he is mistaken. And now, while I think of it, there is a message which I should be glad to send to Mr. Brown, if you will be so kind as to convey it."

I expressed my willingness to carry the message.

"It has probably come to your knowledge that my daughter Caroline has won the admiration of Mr. Brown."

I replied that Anthony had mentioned it.

"The truth is," resumed Mr. Allen, "we entertained the highest opinion of the young man, and he has visited frequently at our house. I am willing to admit to you that the feeling I spoke of has been mutual. With your appreciation of the claims of propriety, the impossibility of a union will of course be apparent to you."

"Then you regard it as impossible?" I asked.

"Yes," he replied. "Do you not so regard it? Think for a moment what it involves. Some friends of ours in a Western city, as my wife was saying yesterday, have had a trouble of this kind a generation or two back, and the children of the present family are in a condition of chronic worry upon the subject. They are wealthy, and are regarded and treated in society as white people; but the two young ladies use some kind of whitening on their faces habitually. The circumstances of the case are pretty generally known, and you can understand how unpleasant such a matter must be to the entire family. It is claimed that a tinge of color sometimes passes over a generation and appears more markedly in the next. I do not know how that may be, but the idea of the risk is enough to give one chills. There is a story that the Western family of which I spoke has a colored grandson concealed somewhere. Of course I do not know whether it is true or not; but it serves as an illustration.

"My message to Mr. Brown is, that, under all the circumstances, we think he should discontinue his visits at our house. I presume he will see that he should take that course. I shall always be glad to meet him anywhere except at my home. In regard to a business engagement, if he will allow me to say a word, I would suggest that he should teach our colored school. They are looking for a teacher just now, as it happens, and he would be very popular in that capacity."

I could not but admit that Mr. Allen's suggestions were characterized by practical wisdom, but I hinted that the course proposed seemed hardly just to Anthony.

"As to that," said Mr. Allen, "it is true that our laws and customs are unjust and cruel in their treatment of a subjugated race. But it is not wrong to avoid marriage with any other race than our own. As to the part that is unjust, you and I cannot remedy that. So far as we are individually concerned, we may deal justly with the downtrodden, and I hope we do so; but the great wrong will still remain."

I left the office of Mr. Allen, feeling that he was in the right. I went directly to Anthony, and, with a heavy heart, reported to him the particulars of the interview. It was a painful shock, but he bore it with greater calmness and fortitude than I had expected. When I had concluded the recital, he remarked sadly that he found it impossible to say that Mr. Allen was wrong, hard as the truth seemed. He felt that marriage was out of the question, and said that he would not have indulged the thought of it if he had reflected upon the matter carefully. He was not fully decided what course he would pursue. It was too painful a subject and involved too great a change to admit of a hasty decision; and he desired my best thoughts and counsel, which I gave him.

After two days I returned to Whitesboro, leaving Anthony in Philadelphia, still pondering the course he would pursue. Three weeks later I received a letter from him, in which he announced that he had taken the colored school.

Four months passed away. Then I received from my friend a long communication, setting forth rather formally his experience in his new position and unfolding to me new views which he had gained by reflection and contact with the world. He also presented the plan of life which he had decided upon, if I approved. I was greatly surprised at the entire revolution in his ideas which had been effected by his observation and his courageous mental struggles.

"My own thoughts," he wrote, "have been completely changed by reading and reflection. There are three aspects of this subject which I wish to make clear to you. There is first the view that every colored man has some sort of strange, mysterious curse resting upon him by a law of his nature. The idea is that, although the black man in any given instance may be superior, spiritually, intellectually, and physically, to his white neighbor, yet he cannot equal him because of this mysterious curse. This view, sad as it is (advocated by the white race), has settled down upon the minds of millions of colored people. It has crushed out of them all self-reliance and independence. It fastens tenaciously upon the quiet, sensitive spirit, destroying its hope and self-respect and enterprise. I need not tell you how near I have come to being shipwrecked by its influence. But it is founded upon a lie. It is a lie backed up by the assertion, practically, of nations and of millions of intelligent persons acting in their individual capacity. It is, however, none the less a base, malignant, falsehood, robbing the spirit that is cowed and crushed by it of the sweetest possessions of life. A similar falsehood has established castes in India, and still another has subjugated woman in many lands, making her a soulless being and the slave of man.

"If any black man has greater wisdom, strength, and goodness than the majority of white men, he is higher in the scale of manhood than they. The real question involved is a comparison of individuals, and not of races.

"You will remember how Homer, in the 'Iliad,' praises the blameless Ethiopians, beloved of the gods and dwelling in a wide land that stretches from the rising to the setting of the sun. The ancient historians praise them also. Words of commendation of this great historic people are found in the ancient classics. So far as

I can discover, the prejudice against color is of modern origin.

"I believe that at no very distant day the slaves will be liberated, and that the Almighty will be the avenger of their wrongs.

"I turn now to consider the second aspect of this subject. When a colored man is wise enough and courageous enough to embrace the views which I have presented, he may still be compelled as a part of his lot in life, to submit to the assumption that he is inferior. It is hard to live in this way in the shadow of a great lie, but it is better than to have the iron enter more deeply into the soul, so as to compel belief of the lie, as is the case with millions of human beings. When the spirit is enfranchised I can understand that one may lead a very noble life in cheerfully submitting to the inevitable misfortune. There are a few colored men who thus recognize the truth and yet bow to the great sorrow, which they cannot escape, with noble and manly fortitude. I confess that I have entertained thoughts of attempting such a life. I think I could do so if I could see that any great good would be accomplished by it. But my experience here has taught me that any such sacrifice is not required of me. I find that it is not to the advantage of the colored people to be taught at present. They tell me that as they grow in knowledge their degradation becomes more apparent to them, and their sufferings greater. They leave the school with the impression that for them ignorance rather than knowledge is the road to happiness. I cannot deny the truth of their reasoning. If they could be raised above the sense of degradation from which they suffer, it would be different. But, apparently, this cannot be done. It is at least impossible in the few years which can be given to their instruction in the schools now provided for their education. The prevailing sentiment among them is against education and in favor of a thoughtless and easy life. They do not wish to face those fires through which the awakened spirit, crushed by hopeless oppression, must necessarily pass. Only yesterday a young man described to me, with thrilling pathos, the anguish of spirit with which he had felt the fetters tightening upon him as his knowledge increased.

"I do not feel called upon, therefore, to devote my life to teaching. If there was hope left in the case, perhaps I might do so. I would labor on willingly if there were light ahead. But, with millions in slavery and others as tightly bound down by prejudice as if they were slaves, I see no encouragement. I think it the wiser course to wait, trusting that Providence will open a way for a change to come. And this brings me to the third aspect of this matter, and the last phase of it which I desire to consider. It seems to me to be my duty and privilege to withdraw from the unequal contest. The stupendous lie which crushes the mass of the colored race has not imposed itself upon me, although I have had a terrible struggle with it that nearly cost me my reason. I am not so situated as to be compelled to live among those whose very presence would be a constant shadow, a burden to me, and a reproach to my existence. Fortunately, I am not compelled to accept the great misfortune and bow to the assumptions of a ruling race. I can retire to the fastnesses of my native hills and forests, where petty distinctions fade away in the majestic presence of nature. I am already beginning to anticipate the change, and instinctively asserting that independence which I feel. Indeed, I have given offense in several instances. I have no trouble with solid business men like Mr. Allen. They have the good sense and fairness to recognize the fact that a man is a man wherever you find him. But some people of the fanciful sort, with less brains than I have, do me the honor to be angry because I do not submit to any assumptions of superiority on their part. I might be so situated that it would be wisdom to submit, to bend to a lie, to lead the life of a martyr, as some noble men of my acquaintance do under such circumstances. But, fortunately, I can afford to be independent, and I shall do so and take the risk of bodily violence.

"You have now my plan of life and my reasons for it. I shall adhere to it under all ordinary circumstances. Nevertheless, if Providence calls me to some work where great good can be done, I will sacrifice my independence and take up the load of misfortune which prejudice imposes, if that is required, and try to bear meekly the burden and do my duty in the battle of life. But I hope this may not be required of me. Around my home, as you know, are many immigrants, foreign-born, who do not inherit or feel the prejudice against color. My family is already one of the wealthiest and most influential in our little community. With such property as I have and can readily gain, and with such school-teaching and political teaching as I can do, it is a settled thing that our standing will be at the head of society and business, so far as we have any such distinctions among us. To refer to the matter of color in a business light, I may remind you that its trace is very faint in our family line. Already it has entirely disappeared in my own person. With wealth and position it will be to me at home as though it were not; and when my dear mother passes away it will disappear entirely and be speedily lost to memory. I do not mean by this to shirk the position of the colored man, of which I have had a bitter taste. I only mean to show you the brightness and hope of my situation. I trust that you will approve of the course which I have marked out, and give me some credit for courage in meeting and conquering the grisly terror, the base lie, which sought to blast my life."

It would be difficult to express too strongly my admiration for my friend as I read the letter from which I have quoted. It seemed to me wonderful that he had been able so to disentangle himself from difficulties. The cool intrepidity with which he had fought his way through those mental troubles which had seemed at one time about to overwhelm him was to me the most astonishing part of the performance. I wrote to him in terms of the highest commendation, frankly expressing my astonishment at the vigor, truth, and force apparent in his actions and his reasoning. He was satisfied with my letter, and proceeded to close up his affairs in a deliberate and decorous manner before returning home and carrying his plan into execution. It was his idea that I should spend some months each year with him and he had made other friends who would be invited to visit him.

For three years only this plan was pursued by us. Matters were as I have described, when the war of the Rebellion broke out. Here was that call to public duty which he had alluded to as a possible interference which might change the course of his life. He felt from the first that the contest was a fight for the black man, and he was anxious to engage in it. In a hasty letter to me he recognized the fact that the spirit of John Brown, whom he greatly admired, was still busy in the affairs of the nation, although his body was sleeping in the grave at North Elba.

Anthony Brown enlisted in a white regiment, there being no trace of color about him and no objection being made. He claimed to have a presentiment that he would fall in battle at an early day. Whether it was a presentiment or a mere fancy, it was his fate. He now rests with the indistinguishable dead

> Where the buzzard, flying,
> Pauses at Malvern Hill.

When I learned of his death, a duty fell upon me. He had written in one of his letters that if he did not return from the war he would like to have me tell his mother the true history of his life. He had concealed from her his struggles in reference to color. She knew nothing of his trials at Whitesboro or at Philadelphia. No words had ever passed between them upon the subject. He thought it better, if he lived, that she should never know, but if he died he wished that his history should be fully made known to her.

I made the journey on horseback over the ground I have already described. It was a delightful autumn day when I passed through the village of Champion and went on to Mrs. Brown's home. She was expecting me, as I had written in advance announcing my intended visit. I could see that she was greatly pleased to receive me. I had been at the house two days before I ventured to introduce, in a formal manner, the subject of my mission. Talking of old times, and leading gradually up to the subject, I frankly stated that Anthony had charged me to tell her the story of his personal history, and I exhibited his letter to her. It was after dinner, as we were sitting in the front room reading and talking. Mrs Brown immediately became excited and anxious to hear. As I disclosed the sorrow of Anthony's life and related the particulars of his career, the effect upon her was not at all what I had expected. She became more and more excited and distressed. At last she called sharply to her servant-girl, Melissa, and told her to go and bring Father Michael, and to bid him come immediately. While Melissa was gone, Mrs. Brown, with a great deal of agitation in her manner, proceeded to question me in regard to the incidents of Anthony's career in Philadelphia, and frequently broke out with the exclamation, "Why could we not have known?"

Soon Father Michael came, and the woman assailed him at once in a harsh and accusing manner, speaking in the French language with great volubility. He replied to her in the same tongue. There was only here and there a word that I could understand. It was plain, however, that there was a contest between them, and that it related to my deceased friend.

By degrees the matter was so far made plain that I understood that Anthony was not the son of Mrs. Brown, but was of the purest white blood and connected with people of rank. Beyond this I was not permitted to know his history. When I asked questions, Father Michael replied that it was better "not to break through the wall of the past." He said it was too late now to aid Anthony, but added that the trouble might have been averted if it had been known at the time.

A day later I took my departure. As I traveled back to Whitesboro I reflected upon the strange events that had shaped Anthony's career. When I turned on the Steuben hills and looked once more upon Castorland, it seemed to me a region of mystery; and the useless tears fell from my eyes as I remembered how one of its secrets had darkened the life of one of the dearest friends of my youth.

I subsequently learned that Miss Allen, of Philadelphia, suffered indirectly from the effects of Anthony's misfortune. She was not able to forget the man she had chosen.

I have never learned the facts in regard to the early history and real parentage of Anthony Calvert Brown.

New York Classics
Frank Bergmann, *Series Editor*

Other titles in the New York Classics series include:
At Midnight on the 31st of March. Josephine Young Case
Bert Breen's Barn. Walter D. Edmonds
The Boyds of Black River: A Family Chronicle. Walter D. Edmonds
Canal Town. Samuel Hopkins Adams
The Civil War Stories of Harold Frederic. Harold Frederic; Thomas F. O'Donnell, ed.
The Color of a Great City. Theodore Dreiser
Drums Along the Mohawk. Walter D. Edmonds
The Genesee. Henry W. Clune
Grandfather Stories. Samuel Hopkins Adams
Half the Way Home: A Memoir of Father and Son. Adam Hochschild
In the Hands of the Senecas. Walter D. Edmonds
In the Wilderness. Charles Dudley Warner
Listen for a Lonesome Drum: A York State Chronicle. Carl Carmer
The Lost Weekend: A Novel. Charles Jackson
Man's Courage. Joseph Vogel
The Mohawk. Codman Hislop
Mostly Canallers. Walter D. Edmonds
My Kind of Country: Favorite Writings About New York. Carl Carmer
Rochester on the Genesee. Blake McKelvey
Rome Haul. Walter D. Edmonds
Stories of Saint Nicholas. James Kirke Paulding
Time to Go House. Walter D. Edmonds
The Traitor and the Spy: Benedict Arnold and John André. James Thomas Flexner
Upstate. Edmund Wilson
A Vanished World. Anne Gertrude Sneller